P9-CIV-558

This is a story of two girls: Erin and Irun. One lives now in New York City, and one belongs in ancient Egypt 3,000 years ago.

For Erin, the "now" she lives in is not all she'd like it to be. There are problems around her and within her that she cannot always understand. She is a loner until a young Egyptian boy, Seti, befriends her. And in her own time, Irun has much the same feelings of discontent, and another Seti tries to understand.

But there are other things that bind the girls—the same appearance, their relationships with their parents, and a cat called Ta-she. Perhaps the two girls are in some way the same person after all.

MARY STOLZ was born in Boston and grew up in New York City, where she attended Columbia University. She is married and lives in Connecticut. Ms. Stolz is the author of over twenty books for young readers; there are Yearling editions of her books *The Bully of Barkham Street, A Dog on Barkham Street, In a Mirror*, and in a Laurel-Leaf Library edition, *Leap Before You Look*.

ALSO AVAILABLE IN LAUREL-LEAF BOOKS:

BUT WE ARE NOT OF EARTH, *Jean Karl*

SATURDAY, THE TWELFTH OF OCTOBER,
Norma Fox Mazer

A WRINKLE IN TIME, *Madeleine L'Engle*

A WIND IN THE DOOR, *Madeleine L'Engle*

A SWIFTLY TILTING PLANET, *Madeleine L'Engle*

THE BOOK OF THREE, *Lloyd Alexander*

THE BLACK CAULDRON, *Lloyd Alexander*

THE CASTLE OF LLYR, *Lloyd Alexander*

TARAN WANDERER, *Lloyd Alexander*

THE HIGH KING, *Lloyd Alexander*

CAT
In the
MIRROR

Mary Stolz

LAUREL-LEAF BOOKS bring together under a single imprint out-standing works of fiction and nonfiction particularly suitable for young adult readers, both in and out of the classroom. Charles F. Reasoner, Professor Emeritus of Children's Literature and Reading, New York University, is consultant to this series.

Published by
Dell Publishing Co., Inc.
1 Dag Hammarskjold Plaza
New York, New York 10017

Copyright © 1975 by Mary Stolz

All rights reserved. No part of this book may be used or reproduced in any manner whatsoever without written permission except in the case of brief quotations embodied in critical articles and reviews. For information address Harper & Row, Publishers, Inc., 10 East 53rd Street, New York, New York 10022.

Laurel-Leaf Library ® TM 766734,
Dell Publishing Co., Inc.

ISBN: 0-440-91123-0

RL: 5.4

Reprinted by arrangement with Harper & Row, Publishers, Inc.

Printed in the United States of America

January 1978

10   9   8   7   6

For Eliza G. Hoskins,
and for O'Hara

PART ONE

PART ONE

CHAPTER ONE

"Erin, you're making faces again. Erin!"

"What did you say? I didn't hear you."

"You don't hear because you don't *want* to hear. I *said* you are making faces again."

"What faces?"

"Erin. You know what I'm talking about. You're blowing out your cheeks again. I just cannot understand *why* you *do* that."

"It stretches my skin. It feels good."

"It looks simply frightful."

"I know."

"Then why do you do it?"

"I don't know."

She did not know why she did it—blew out first one side of her face, then the other, then made a big sort of bubble around her mouth and popped the air out with what *she* called a vulgar noise. Sometimes she opened her eyes as wide as they'd go. It did feel good, did look dreadful, and in spite of telling *her* she only did it at home in her own room, she knew she made faces, without thinking, at school. The kids laughed at her about it. *Blowfish Gandy*, they called her, not always behind her back. She didn't seem to be able to stop.

Now Mrs. Gandy let the matter drop and said, "Daddy and I are going away for a few days, lambie. You won't mind that, will you?"

Lambie, sweetie-pie. All those pet names she used. Erin didn't know who she thought she was fooling. Anyway, not me, Erin thought, stroking Posey, taking great interest in her markings. A calico cat, with a bushy tail and a fondling nature.

She loves being on my lap, Erin thought. Loves having me rub her beautiful ears. Hear how she purrs.

"Sweetie, I'm *talking* to you."

Erin stroked the cat's chin and admitted to herself that of course Posey would lie on any lap presented to her, accept any stroking hand. She was an affectionate animal, obviously trusting and used to being loved. Not the *bright*est cat, maybe, that ever came down the pike, but—

"Oh, very well," said Mrs. Gandy. "If you want to *sulk*, there's nothing *I* can do about it."

"I'm not sulking."

"You give every appearance of it. You behave as if you found the *cat* more interesting than what I'm trying to tell you."

Oh, but I do. Definitely, I do.

"I was just thinking how friendly she is."

"That's been remarked upon sufficiently, I think. You must get out of the habit of re*peat*ing, love. It makes you sound so limited." She glanced at the cat

12

and shook her head. "The things I do for that sister of mine. I'll certainly be glad when she gets back."

Erin, who'd been trying to work out a plea for a cat of her own when Posey got returned to Aunt Marthe, abandoned hope. She'd been lucky to have Posey for the month that Aunt Marthe had been in Europe, but what she really wanted was a cat of her own. Not Posey, who was eight years old and very *settled*. Erin thought that probably even as a kitten Posey hadn't been a real frisker. For a cat she was strangely unadventurous. The only condition under which Mrs. Gandy had agreed to have her at all was that she share Erin's room and bath and be kept away from the rest of the house. But Posey hadn't shown the least interest in the rest of the house. She'd moved into Erin's quarters and settled down like an old lady in a good nursing home. She had her litter box and food and water dishes in Erin's bathroom. She slept on Erin's bed, whether Erin was in it or not. No roving, no scratching at the door, no mewing for the missing Aunt Marthe. Food, sleep, a gentle hand—anyone's gentle hand—that was what Posey looked for in life.

In fact, thought Erin, Posey is a beauty without much personality. What I want is a kitten, lively and wild and *aware* of things. Imagining how *she* would react to the idea of such a pet, Erin sighed and transferred her gaze from Posey on her lap to the woman in the pink velvet chair.

"Do you even know what I said?" Mrs. Gandy asked.

"That you and Daddy are going away. Again."

"Oh, my *word*. You'd think your father and I whirled around the world on a weekly basis."

"Daddy practically does."

"That's his *job*. Certainly *I* don't get away very often. Look at your Aunt Marthe. A whole month in the south of France and I'll bet she'll be off again before too long and asking us to take the *cat* again. *Why* the thing can't stay at a veterinarian's is more than I can—"

"Animals suffer at a veterinarian's," Erin interrupted. "Especially cats."

"How do you know so much about cats?"

"I don't know how I do, I just do. Besides, Posey isn't any trouble to you."

"No, no. I realize that, and that you've been very good with her."

"Anyway, Aunt Marthe doesn't have a family."

"What does that have to do with anything? You mean that's why she keeps a cat?"

"I mean that's why it's okay for her to travel so much. You were away last month with Daddy."

"For a week. Really. Do you begrudge us a little pleasure now and then? Does that *really* seem too much to ask?"

"You could take me with you sometimes."

"We've taken you with us. Quite often. And, of course, we shall again."

"'Jam tomorrow and jam yesterday—but never jam today.'"

"What's that?"

"It's from *Alice in Wonderland*. It's really from *Through the Looking Glass*. It doesn't matter where it's from, it still comes out to 'Jam tomorrow and jam yester—'"

"Erin, stop feeling so sorry for yourself. It gives you such a *peevish* expression. Besides, you're a *very* lucky girl. You have—"

As her blessings were counted for her Erin stopped

listening. She could do this easily, like a deaf person turning off a hearing aid. She switched on again after a while. "When you grow up, you'll find that grown-ups need to be *alone* together sometimes. It's the most natural thing in the world for your father and me to want to be *away*, just the two of us, from time to time. You'll see how it is when you grow up and have a husband of your own."

If I'm the dog you think I am, Erin thought, how am I going to get a husband? I think maybe I'd better carve out a rewarding career. "I'm not going to," she said.

"You're not going to what?"

"Grow up."

"Oh, my goodness." Mrs. Gandy had a light pretty laugh. People remarked on it. They said, "What a light pretty laugh Belle Gandy has." She was now laughing her light pretty laugh. "What are you going to be, love, a female Peter *Pan?*"

"Who's that?"

"You mean to tell me you've never read *Peter Pan?*"

"I started it. It was dopey."

"But then you do know who he was. Why did you say 'Who's that?' Don't be sly, Erin. It's *so* unattractive."

What was a synonym for unattractive? There really had to be one. "I don't care if I'm unattractive."

"Now, that *is* an asinine thing to say. You are *obliged* to care if you're unattractive."

"Why?"

Mrs. Gandy rose. "Erin, you are simply impossible when you get in these moods, and I will *not* continue the conversation until you can be reasonable. The cat's scratching the velvet on the chair. Did you notice that?" She leaned over and frowned at the cushion where certainly there were a few picked threads of velvet. Erin had meant to turn the cushion around but had, naturally, forgotten.

"The animal should be declawed. I can't think why Marthe doesn't—"

Erin jumped to her feet, tumbling an unastonished Posey to the carpet. "That's a wicked cruel horrible thing to say! How would you like to have your fingernails pulled out, how would *that* feel?"

"Stop *shriek*ing. I don't claw people's furniture, so there is no reason for me to—"

"Suppose she got out sometime by accident? How would she protect herself? A cat's claws are *part* of her. You don't tear off part of a person so that your damned furniture will be smooth!"

"She's not a person, and stop swearing. And stop carrying on like a public defender. I make a simple suggestion and you turn it into a federal case. There are times when you act so melodramatic and misused that it's—embarrassing, that's what it is." She went toward the door. In anyone else it would have been a stride, but she managed to make it wafting. "It seems to me," she said, turning, her hand on the porcelain doorknob, "that every time you and I are together for ten minutes, we get into some awful stupid pointless argument. I should think you'd be *glad* to have me away for a few days."

She was gone, quietly closing the door behind her.

"Well, I am glad," Erin muttered, sitting in the velvet chair and scowling at the floor. As she'd expected, Posey sauntered over and leaped up to reoccupy her lap.

"I don't mind having *her* gone," Erin explained. "It's

just that I'd like to be with Daddy sometimes." Posey lifted placid amber eyes and fixed them on Erin's, dark and brooding. She seemed to study Erin's face, framed by a tangle of dark hair, cut with bangs and falling in tight ripples halfway down her back. Posey regarded the girl and seemed to find nothing remarkable. She fell asleep.

Erin picked up one of the immaculate paws, gently pressing so that the curved translucent claws emerged. She shuddered. It would be worse, really, than tearing out a person's nails. It would be chopping off fingers and toes. Was *she* really unable to feel what another creature—a cat, a child—felt?

After a while she reached to the night table and picked up *Alice in Wonderland*. This was the second time she'd read it. Her father loved it. He often quoted from it and reread parts from time to time. He couldn't believe she didn't feel as he did, so here she was, second time around, trying to love it. It was the crossest book she'd ever read in her life. Full of creatures with unpleasant dispositions and nasty habits. Everyone snapping and snarling at everybody else. Duping and deceiving, interrupting, threatening, contradicting. Not one nice or agreeable party in the whole thing and Alice the worst of all, except for being the only one who made sense at that horrible trial of the knave of hearts.

Well, the book suited her mood at the moment. " 'You're nothing but a pack of *cards*!' said Alice."

"That's what they all are, the whole entire world," said Erin to an unheeding Posey. "Nothing but a stupid pack of cards."

CHAPTER TWO

For a week Erin spent most of her time with Flora Todd, their housekeeper. They ate in the kitchen together, sat in the living room in the evening looking at television, went marketing, walked in Central Park.

"Pretty soon," Flora said one day as they returned from an afternoon at the zoo, "you'll be going back to Bramley-Wade. It'll be good for you to see your schoolmates again, now won't it?"

Erin felt a flash of panic. With the cooperation of her conscious and unconscious, she had somehow managed to hold off, bury, forget, be unaware of the approach of the school year. Now Flora had thrown it at her when her defenses were down, along with a snippet of the fantasy she and Erin's mother entertained about "schoolmates." What a word.

Oh, God, they're so stupid, Erin thought. Stupid. "What schoolmates?" she wanted to yell. "What are you *talking* about? Do I ever get invited to anybody's house? Does anybody ever get invited to my house?

Why do you suppose that is, you dopes, you dumb-bells? Nobody *likes* me, that's why."

But after that time in France, she'd never said the words aloud again. Actually, she was pretty sure she'd throw up if she said them. Sickening enough to know it and not know why. Did she talk too much, laugh too much? Make fools' faces too much? Push herself *in* too much? That might have been true, that last, about schools in the past, but *not* since France. At Bramley-Wade she'd scarcely said a word all last year, her first year there. Oh, she'd tried a few times to be part of things, only it came out the same at Bramley-Wade as it had at other schools. She'd read in a book once that there is always somebody in a class, or an office, or an institution—anyplace—who is somehow more teas-able than the rest of the people. That's me, she thought. Teasable Erin Gandy. Step right up, folks, and watch her lose her head.

Of course, she wasn't absolutely alone in her posi-tion. But in a world where there were Ins, Semi-Ins, Semi-Outs, and Outs, she fell, wherever she went, into her proper category like a computer card. In the same slot in her class at Bramley-Wade were Roby Watson and Eloise Marx. Roby was cheerful, even exuberant (or tried so hard to be that he practically was), unless surrounded by that Pack of Ins led by Fred Englund. Eloise was a nice girl. Shy. Erin was also cheerful. Sometimes. Almost. Shy, too. Inclined to lose her head, of course.

But they—she and Eloise and Roby—were okay peo-ple. As okay, as far as she could see, as—say—the Semi-Ins. So why did they get singled out to be Outs? The kind who made the Pack bristle and close in? They were teasable, that was why. Roby would lose his vivacity and grow silent, sullen. Eloise would cry. She herself would lose her cool and scream.

"I remember the first day of school as if it were yesterday," Flora was going on. "The lovely smell of new clothes and new books, and seeing old friends and making new—"

"Did you have to remind me?" Erin yelled and ran upstairs to her room, where she gathered Posey to her and struggled not to cry.

"See here," she said aloud to the cat. "Look here. Don't you think there's a good chance I'm exaggerating? People my age, you know, exaggerate something awful. Well, you wouldn't know, but they do. We do. It's something to do with some awful word—pubescent— which actually *awfully* means getting *body* hair. That's something you wouldn't know anything about, either, having come with all your body hair on you."

Alice had had the right idea, talking to her cats. It was soothing or something. Reassuring. Silly, of course. But very very helpful if you didn't really have anyone else to talk to. She had her father. When he was home. But she wouldn't tell him things like this. What could he do about it, except get sad? Or tell her, as he'd tried to tell her in France that time, that she was exaggerating. Which was just what she was telling herself. Or telling Posey, who could be relied upon not to be saddened or to offer advice. You couldn't talk out loud to yourself, but talking to a cat seemed pretty natural.

"I wish," she said, "that people came with their body hair on. Fur on. Fur is a much nicer word. Nicer material, come to that." She ran her finger gently down Posey's nose, going with the fur, over and over. Posey crooned. But wouldn't that have been lovely, if people had been designed to be born with fur. No need to bother about clothes. Just wear a few jewels from time to time, if you felt like it. Race wouldn't matter, color wouldn't matter, age wouldn't show. Anyway not nearly so badly and baldly. No cat would ever look the way her great-grandfather Gandy had looked before he died. Long before he died.

When she'd been a little girl, Erin had gone with her father to the big house in Virginia where the old man had lived with two male nurses who took care of him. He'd been over ninety then, with a skin wrinkled and brown as a dried apricot and faded blue eyes that had fixed on hers with a glance like a skewer. He'd had a thin, sharp voice and a thin, still-tough body, although he'd needed the help of his nurses to get about, and there'd been a strong odor about him that her father later said was Myer's dark rum.

"You're Brian?" he'd said to Peter Gandy. "About time you got here."

"No, Grandfather. I'm Peter, Brian's son. And this is Erin, my daughter. You remember when we brought her here. She was just a baby then."

"Don't remember a thing about that. Where's Brian?"

"Father died five years ago, Grandfather."

"Did he. Beat me to it, then."

"I'm afraid so."

"Afraid. Well, you may be, but I'm not. Can't wait, if you want the fact." He thrust out his arm toward the nurse, who'd put a small glass of dark liquid and chipped ice into his talonlike hand. "Who's she?"

"Erin. My daughter. Your great-granddaughter."

"Get her out of here. She shouldn't be around all this decay. Out!"

She and her father had stayed overnight, and Erin hadn't gone back to the overheated shadowy odorous room. She'd wandered the grounds, feeding some geese and ducks in the little lake, climbing trees, waiting to go home. She'd been pretty young but able to read well already, and she remembered she'd been reading *Stuart Little* and that had helped to take her away from the feeling of terror and sadness that the house and the old man filled her with. She'd left her light on all night, and the next day after lunch, when her father had said they were leaving, she'd almost yelled with relief. Almost, not quite.

On the drive home, her father had said, "Maybe it was a mistake to take you, Erin. I know it was hard on you."

"No. Well, a little. But I wanted to come with you. I *love* taking a trip with you."

"It's been fun, hasn't it? Except for—" He stopped, shrugging. When there was nothing to say, her father didn't use words trying to say it.

"Does he drink all that rum because he's in pain?"

Her father had nodded and then said, "Look, Erin! Look at that wisteria vine that's covered the entire telegraph pole!"

He'd slowed so they could see the thick and towering vine, so heavy with blossoms that almost no green showed through the purple clusters.

Her great-grandfather had lived for another seven years, but she never saw him again.

"Animals," her father had said when he came back from the funeral, "have these things better arranged."

"Animals," Erin said now to Posey, "seem to me to have everything better arranged."

Animals died when their time came, and meanwhile

they didn't bother with clothes, or go to war, or get drunk, or judge other animals by their looks. They didn't get afraid unless there was something to be afraid of. She herself often came apart with terror over something she couldn't define or understand. She didn't get afraid of *something*. She just got terrified. Filled with anxiety. For no reason. For no reason she could name. Would name.

Animals didn't look back with shivering shame at things in their past. They didn't quake at the thought of what lay ahead. They didn't try to make it into a clique and feel sick with humiliation because they couldn't make it. Some animals, of course, had a pecking order, but they just pecked along in the proper order and probably didn't feel they'd lost face for that reason. Cats, naturally, had no such matter in their lives.

"Pecking order, indeed," she said to Posey. "Do you realize that you belong to the proudest, securest species in the world? No, of course you don't realize it, because if you thought about things like that you'd belong to some other species. Human, it's called."

Posey purred and licked her hand in a friendly way.

"Oh, God," said Erin. "I wish I didn't have to go to school."

CHAPTER THREE

"Why don't we take a picnic and go over to see Shakespear in the Park," Mr. Gandy said one afternoon. "They're doing *Antony and Cleopatra,* and it should be great."

Mrs. Gandy looked at him indulgently. "You and Egypt. You're an archeologist *manqué,* that's what you are."

"What's *manqué*?" Erin asked.

"Missed," Mr. Gandy said, when his wife didn't reply. "A person *manqué*—something or other—is one who missed what he was really meant to be and became something else, *faute de mieux.*"

"What's *faute de mieux*?"

"Two years in France," said Belle Gandy. "Would you believe it?"

Peter Gandy rubbed the back of his neck. "Your mother is teasing me again," he said, "because of that time I went to Egypt with a friend who *was* an archeologist and was allowed to poke about in the digs where I couldn't do any harm. That's where I found that beautiful piece of ostraca they finally let me buy and take out of the country."

It was one of his great treasures. A little piece of limestone on which some long-forgotten artist had sketched a tiny hippopotamus coming out of the river. There were stalks of papyrus near the hippo's shoulder and a little bird on his head. Her father said this lovely thing was probably a doodle, done by the artist and tossed away. There were, he said, numberless such pieces lying just under the surface of the earth wherever the kings and nobles of Egypt had been buried or had their temples built.

"Egypt is dazzling," he said. "The remains of the ancient land, that is. Not modern Egypt, of course."

"Why 'of course'?"

"There are no dazzling countries anymore. Not in the sense I mean. But I got the feeling, looking at the remains of tombs and temples, spending hours in the Cairo Museum, that it must've been a country full of artists—way back then, thousands of years ago. In Thebes, in the Valley of the Kings and the Valley of the Nobles, there are wall paintings that would drive a Picasso mad with envy. And the sculpture—that massive, ponderous, *calm* sculpture. I stood there at Abu Simbel with such a sense of just the right kind of awe that I felt maybe I'd lived there way back then."

"Your ancestors," Belle Gandy said, "are Scots back to the Picts."

"Just the same," said Mr. Gandy with a smile, "that's the feeling I got."

"Besides, all your paintings and sculpture were the result of slave labor. Slave labor and death worship. Awful."

"Belle, you know I don't believe that. Nothing so splendid could be the result of slave labor. I've never believed it since I was there. People can't be impressed or beaten into creating beauty."

"So far as I can make out, all your ancient Egyptians did was crawl about getting ready to die. I ask you, what's left of their *civilization* besides tombs and temples?"

"What's survived is what they built in durable materials. Limestone and granite last. They built their houses of mud bricks, and from all we've been able to discover, they were enchanting houses indeed. Colorful, spacious, with gardens and pools and sanitary facilities. More than my Scottish ancestors could boast of for thousands of years to come."

"The rich, you're speaking of."

He nodded. "Have to. Have the poor thrived in any land, in any time? I'd say the Egyptian poor probably made out better than many. They had sun, and a river brimming with fish, the richest soil in the world to grow their produce in."

"And a pharaoh driving them to death so that he could survive forever."

"Oh well, Belle. There's no arguing with that point of view. It's been held for centuries and some Egyptologists hold it still, but most do not, and I come down on the side of the majority in this instance. I prefer to think, since I have the option, that it was a colorful, rather polished world. They rarely did battle, stopped killing their captives long before other nations did—"

"They kept slaves."

"Who could be freed. Who could own land and marry whom they wished."

Belle Gandy shook her head and smiled at her husband, enfolded him in her smiling regard. "All right," she said, as if granting him a point he hadn't earned. "You keep your dream of Egypt, Peter. A land full of people who were so in love with life that all they thought about was death—"

"Because they knew that life was short and death was long and they really did believe that the next world was a marvelously refined, unending version of this world. Naturally they wanted to be well prepared for the journey there. As simple as your making sure you have the clothes and jewels you'll want on a trip to Europe. I think that the ancient Egyptians preparing for death were livelier and more colorful than a lot of people living for the moment."

"You are *hopeless*," she said, laughing. "How a grown man can cling to a vision in this way—"

"Plenty of grown men called historians and archeologists cling to visions. Some of them must be right."

"Of course, darling. Of course."

She doesn't care if the Egyptians kept slaves or lived forever or ever lived at all, Erin thought. What she minds about Egypt is that Daddy was there without her, it was something important in his life before she came into it. She'd like to think he'd never done anything, seen or felt anything, never lived at *all* until she came along. She'd like him to have sprung full-grown at the moment of their meeting.

She wondered if her father had forgotten about *Antony and Cleopatra* but didn't ask. When her parents were talking together, anything she said would be an interruption.

Sometimes she listened to kids at school go on about their parents, or she saw other parents at times when they visited school for the Christmas play, things like that, and she never got the impression that anybody else's were like hers. Were like—were practically like *lovers*. Always having something to say to each other, always wanting to be together. When her father was on a trip he called home every night. He wrote letters to her mother. He did, of course, write to Erin too. He was a darling, thoughtful father.

Mostly he's a husband, Erin thought. She studied them broodingly. You'd think it'd be just super, having parents who you knew would never have horrible loud fights, or quiet little mean fights. Who would certainly never get divorced. So, it was super. It was also—well, no point defining. If she'd had a brother or a sister, or maybe both, that would have been a help. A sister would be best. Someone to share a room with, a point of view with. But she couldn't imagine *her* with two children. Actually, not even with one. She's just not a maternal type, Erin thought, and probably I was an accident that they decided not to do anything about.

Sometimes she wondered if she really wished they *had* done something about it. "Peter darling," she could hear *her* saying, "why do we go through with this? Why bring a third person into our perfect world of two?" Yes, she could think that and find it a reasonable fancy, and probably she owed her life to her father. "Belle, I want us to have this child," he'd have said. "I want to have a daughter who looks just like you." And then *she* would have said, "Oh no, it must be a boy who looks just like you." Hah. Little did they suspect what a nasty surprise was in store for them. Surprise, surprise. It's a baby girl and she looks *just* like her Daddy. After all, she'd turned out to have her mother's long eyes and long neck. But that crisp curly black hair, that sharp strong nose and proud jaw, those were like Peter's and on him looked marvelous, were not to be improved upon. On me, Erin thought, it all comes out to a tragedy.

It was hard to imagine yourself not here, not alive, since that was what had happened and here you were. But she wished sometimes that *she* had had that baby boy, in which case this would be his problem and none of hers.

Oh hell, she thought. Oh damn. Oh *shit*. That helped a little, but not much. She wondered if saying the words aloud would help more but looked at her parents and declined the test. Her mother would look pained, or sick. Her father would look concerned. And it would concentrate their attention on her in a way she didn't wish to earn it.

"What about *Antony and Cleopatra?*" she said loudly.

"Darling, do try to lower your voice, try not to be *shrill.*"

"*Antony and Cleopatra* still strikes me as the best idea I've had today. Not my period, of course, the Ptolemies. I don't go much past the Eighteenth Dynasty. Well, say the Nineteenth—"

"Peter, really, I cannot traipse over to the park with food in a basket and sit on the sour grass to eat it and then sit on a hard chair for hours, or a *bench* more likely. Not even for Shakespear. Not even for you. If you want to go to the theatre, there are lots of good things in *proper* theatres."

"But I want to see *Antony and Cleopatra*, and that's in the park."

"Will you really martyr me to mosquitos and a back-ache and a picnic in the grass?"

"You don't have to go at all. I'll take Erin."

Belle Gandy's dark eyes darkened further, but she nodded and said, "Well, of course. Except that I don't think *Antony and Cleopatra* is quite suitable for some-one Erin's age. She wouldn't understand the nuances. Or I hope she wouldn't."

"Belle, nobody's too young to get started on Shake-spear. My parents started taking me when I was six."

"And a dandy little handful I'll bet you were, teeth-ing on *King Lear*." She smiled and put her hand on his, squeezing and then lightly letting go.

"They held off on Lear until I was eight. How about it, Erin? Want to come? Have you ever seen any Shakespear?"

"The seniors gave *Twelfth Night* last year. And I saw that ballet, *Midsummer Night's Dream*, remem-ber?"

"That's right. But Shakespear set to music and danced isn't the real thing. You know, it's as hard to get an answer out of you as it is to get one from your mother. Do you want to come or don't you?"

"Sure I do, Daddy. I'd love to."

Flora had packed them a picnic in the pretty wicker hamper Mrs. Gandy had bought at Abercrombie's, and Mr. Gandy took all the stuff out of it and put it in a brown paper bag. "Simplify, simplify, as our friend Thoreau advised. We can just throw everything in a litter basket when we're finished."

"But there are two Thermos bottles," Flora pointed out. "Mrs. Gandy said I should make iced tea, and a small Thermos of martinis for you. She said you'd need them."

"Well, I won't. Thanks anyway, Flora. We'll get Cokes or something in the park. Why don't you come along with us?"

"Thank you, Mr. Gandy, but I'm in the middle of my peach chutney."

If it hadn't been chutney, Erin thought, it would've been something else. Flora knew, even if her father didn't, what it meant to Erin to have him to herself. She gave the housekeeper a grateful glance over her shoulder and went off with her father to Central Park to mingle with the crowds, some sprawling on the grass, some sitting on folding chairs they'd brought along, some strolling, all there for the purpose of hearing great words in the Delacorte Theatre. And maybe, Erin thought, yawning at some point in Act Four when Caesar and his soldiers were yakking at one another, maybe in a way *she* had been right. Some of this was pretty boring.

She looked up at the sky and thought how when she'd been a very little girl she'd thought the stars were holes in the sky and that heaven, above the sky, was shining through the holes. A nice sort of idea, she still thought. Now she knew that the light seen from the stars had been traveling thousands, maybe millions of years, to reach Earth. Maybe, she thought, trying to yawn without opening her mouth, maybe the light from some of these stars I'm looking at now started earthward when these people—well, not these actors, but the real Caesar and Cleopatra and Mark Antony and Iras—were walking in their beautiful palace in Alexandria, beside the Nile. Maybe—

Her head fell against her father's shoulder and she slept.

At intermission he said perhaps it would be better

if they went home. "Don't mistake me, Erin. I'm not annoyed in the least. It's just that perhaps this *is* a bit too much for your first real bite of Shakespear."

"Oh, please, Daddy. Please, I don't want to go. I really truly *love* it, especially the parts where Cleopatra is in it."

Her father smiled. "She bewitches down the ages, does she not?"

"She's marvelous. And Mark Antony, too. It's just that Caesar gets a little—"

"Doesn't he? Well then, if you're sure."

"I'm sure."

Walking home when the play had ended, Erin was still wiping tears from her eyes. It had been so *beautiful*. So beautiful and sad. Antony dying in Cleopatra's arms. He'd called her "Egypt." "I am dying, Egypt, dying. . . ." And when he died, Cleopatra lifted her face to the sky and said—

"'The odds are gone, and there is nothing remarkable left beneath the wandering moon,'" Erin murmured aloud.

"The odds is gone, and there is nothing left remarkable beneath the visiting moon," said Mr. Gandy. "You have a remarkable memory."

"I guess there are some things you couldn't forget. Thank you, Daddy. For—"

"I know." He took her hand, swung it lightly, let it go.

Aunt Marthe returned from France. Mr. and Mrs. Gandy gave a party for her. The next day she took Posey and drove back to Greenwich, Connecticut, where they lived, and Mr. Gandy flew to London, taking his wife with him, since, as they explained to Erin, *she* hadn't been to London in ages and besides it was only going to be a quick trip, she'd hardly know they were gone.

All at once it was the night before the first day of school, and it had, as usual, happened too fast. The summer had come and gone. Posey had come and gone. Her parents came and went all the time. And Erin, who could never be induced to go to camp, had stayed where she was, in their brownstone on East Seventy-seventh Street. As in years past, no matter where they'd been living, it had seemed at the beginning of summer that it would go on forever, and then before she'd had time to grasp a moment in her hand, it was over and she had to go back to school.

"Someday," she said to herself, lying in the dark, missing Posey, afraid of the coming day, "sometime, someday, *I'm* going to take a trip. A long one. Really long. Away from here, away from school, away from *her*, away from all all *all* of it. I don't know where I'm going, but one day I'll be on my way."

CHAPTER FOUR

When Erin Gandy had first come to Bramley-Wade, she'd already been to five other schools in three different countries, and in all of them she'd been miserable. But France had been—had been—

Thinking about the school in France still made her skin flush and moisten with shame. She'd gone to a boarding school there. One day Madame Guillet had discovered that her desk had been rifled, papers rearranged, a test paper probably copied. She'd assembled the girls and told them of her discovery and of how disappointed she was.

"*Je suis au désespoir*," Madame had said, looking at them all with despair indeed. She'd said, "If any of you knows who perpetrated this disgraceful act, I feel that I should be informed. I suppose that, in the way of children, you will all stick together and suppose yourselves honorable thereby, but the truth is there would be more honor in helping me to root out such an evil tendency in one—or more—of you. If I knew who had done it, perhaps I could *help* that person, find out *why* she was driven to such debasement. Of course, it would be best if the perpetrator herself—or themselves—should elect to confess to me, and we could work together. But if someone else knows who did it—why, it would be not an act of cowardice but an act of courage and friendship to reveal this knowledge."

Erin had known who'd gone into the desk and copied the test paper and passed it around to certain of her friends. She'd lain all night, thinking about what Madame had said, and the next day had gone after class to whisper the name of the desk rifler in Madame's ear. Why, she asked herself miserably, sickly, later on, had she *whispered*? It had made it all so much horribly worse. *Why* had she done it? *Please, why?*

It was three years past and she still did not know the answer to that, still could not remember the time without shriveling inside. Had she believed what Madame said about its being an act of friendship and courage to peach on another girl? Had she believed she'd been helping to put a poor unfortunate on the road to right-doing again? Had she? Had she hoped to make Madame *like* her, pay attention to her?

Madame hadn't liked her from the first day she'd come to the school. Erin had told her parents so, and Mrs. Gandy had said, "Stop being so self-pitying and self-important, Erin. If you imagine people don't like you, why, pretty soon they won't." And her father, more preoccupied than usual with setting up the new office, had said that, *au fond*, the French didn't tend to rally round citizens of the U.S.A. and she should just ignore it. That was okay for them, but they hadn't been boarding at the school.

Well, she never would know why she'd done it and wished she could stop thinking about it. She thought about it less now, but from time to time it came into her dreams, or even her waking thoughts. She would see again how Madame had looked at her for a long, long time, one tapering red-tipped finger tapping her cheek, and had finally smiled a long slow smile and said, "What a nasty little creature you are, to be sure."

Three years later she sickened with shame, remembering. And she'd had two months more to go at the school. She'd begged her parents to take her out, but since she couldn't tell them, could not ever tell anyone, the reason why, they'd refused. And so she'd stuck it out. Two months of silent hell. And that was no exaggeration, no dramatization, as her mother always said she exaggerated and dramatized. It had been hell.

After that there'd been the year in San Francisco, then two years in Brazil, and now here. Bramley-Wade. Nothing would ever be as bad as France again. But would, sometime, something be good for her? Not just all right, but—*lovely*?

Erin's father, Peter Gandy, was a proper sort of parent for a Bramley-Wade student, where the parents of just about everybody were "important." There were fathers, and mothers, too, who were of consequence in the arts, in politics, in business. Bramley-Wade bristled with the offspring of Names.

Peter Gandy was president of a drug company that specialized in selling hormones for livestock. He had offices all over the world, which he visited regularly. When he set up a new one, he and his wife and Erin would move to the country and stay there while he got it going. Which was how Erin had come to spend a year in Paris and two in Rio de Janeiro, and before that, times in London and in Holland that she remembered only sketchily.

Belle Montgomery Gandy was not one of the mothers who had careers, or sat on boards, or even played outstanding golf. Belle just was. Slender, fresh-skinned, hair black as crows' feathers, face simply beautiful, gorgeously dressed. There she was. Unliberated, as she sometimes said, and proud of it. She wouldn't open a piece of mail addressed to her as *Ms.*, saying, "I am Mrs. Peter Gandy, and that's all I am or wish to be." And she would say, when the subject of women's liberation came up, which was unavoidable from time to time, "*If* I were the joining sort of woman—though nothing could *induce* me to join an organization that *demanded* things, because I am by nature undemanding—but *if*, just as a postulation, I should join a women's group, it would be one on the order of Prevent Equal Rights and Preserve Unequal Advantages. *I* want doors opened for me and men to stand up when I come into a room. I want to get my way by *crying*, not by going through the courts or picketing men's clubs."

Most of the time her hearers seemed to mistake this honest statement for a witticism.

"What are you laughing at?" Erin wanted to ask. "She's absolutely serious."

Erin thought her father looked uncomfortable when Belle spoke this way. He never said anything. And maybe I'm imagining, Erin would go on to herself. Maybe he adores being doted on in this quaint and antiquated fashion.

Her father, when he was around, when he had time, took Erin out. Ice skating in Central Park in the winter, to the museums, which they both loved—the Egyptian Wing at the Metropolitan Museum, the Museum of Natural History. "Do you realize," he'd say, managing to sound awed each time, "that dinosaurs roamed this earth for a *hundred million years*, and the only thing they achieved was extinction? And in fifty years we human beings with our achievements have just about brought the planet to a standstill?" He'd stand, shaking his head, staring up at the dinosaur as if trying to read a message in its bones.

Sometimes they just went for walks, looking in the windows of shops and galleries, just talking. She loved conversations with her father.

"Do you ever," she'd ask, edging up to a discussion of her personal difficulties, "think that life is—awfully hard?"

"I certainly do," he'd say. "Be a peculiar thing if I didn't. Why? Is there something that you're finding especially hard, Erin?"

But she'd retreat, wishing he wouldn't *ask* her if there was something wrong, but would tell her that he knew there was and why didn't they talk about it and maybe he could help. But maybe that was asking too much of another person. After all, he couldn't look in her mind, could he? *Why couldn't he?* Confused at her thoughts, ashamed of them, she'd mutter, "Oh, no—it's just that sometimes things seem *ir*ritating."

"Well, now, we oysters don't make our pearls without some irritation, you know. And agitation, and even pain."

"Yeah—if you could be sure you were making a pearl."

"You are, Missy. You are *becoming* a pearl."

38

When he'd said that, she'd flushed with love and her eyes had brimmed. She loved it when he called her Missy. Loved talking with him, no matter what they said. Or didn't say. The trouble being that there were so few of these times because he not only had to be home and free, she had to be alone with him. When he was with his wife, he just naturally turned to her.

Which is how it should be, Erin would tell herself repeatedly and never become convinced.

"Maybe if I was *attractive*," she said to Flora, pronouncing the word as *she* would, "then maybe things would be different."

"What things?" Flora said reproachfully. "Anyway, you're attractive in your own special way. Everybody can't look like your mother."

"I am not attractive and you know it and don't say things to *pacify* me, Flora. Oh, well, it doesn't matter anyway. All she has to do is stick me in a closet or stay out of my way and after a while I'll grow up and she can tell me it'll be *good* for me to be out on my *own* since I'm so fond of the *liberated* life, and why don't I try maybe New Zealand, it's supposed to be such an *interesting* country—"

"Stop that kind of talk, Erin, you hear me? Your mother doesn't stick you in a closet. You go saying things like that and people might believe you."

"She never takes me anywhere with her—"

"Who's *she*, the cat's mother?"

"You know, Flora, I think sometimes you forget how old I am. You've been saying that to me since I was three."

"And you've been calling your mother *she* or *her*

since you were three. It isn't nice. Besides, you two were out together just the other day. You got a lot of lovely clothes and had luncheon out."

"We didn't have luncheon, we had lunch. In the Bird Cage at Lord & Taylor. And all the time she was buying me clothes, I got this feeling she'd have liked to pretend I wasn't hers at all. She'd have liked to explain to people that I was some Fresh Air kid she was being charitable to but nothing to do with *her*, of course, except that of course she thinks she's above caring what a salesperson in Lord & Taylor's would think, except she isn't, you know. She's ashamed of me and cares what everybody thinks. She didn't really want me to come down to the party she gave for Aunt Marthe, you know, but—"

"Erin! Stop this instant!"

"I won't stop. She just hates not having a gorgeous classy glossy daughter that she could dress up and show off and be proud of—like most of the girls at Bramley-Wade. Any one of them, practically, would make a better daughter for her. Even sniffly Eloise. Sniffly Eloise is pretty, at least. Did you ever notice that rich people usually are better looking than poor people?"

"They eat better food and buy better clothes and keep their teeth and bodies in good shape. They just don't have so many worries. Why shouldn't they be better looking?"

"Because it isn't fair."

"Oh, well, if you're going to go talking about *fair*."

"Wouldn't you like things to be fair, Flora?"

"What I would like has nothing to do with the price of cheese."

"I suppose that's what everybody says. Maybe it's

why things go on being unfair. I think everything ought to be divided up all over the world. Including worries."

"If everything was divided up, you can be sure you wouldn't be living in this house or having me to wait on you hand and foot."

Erin giggled. " 'Hand and foot.' You're funny. No, just the same—I wouldn't care. I mean, I'd miss *you* and all, but maybe we could visit. Or I could wait on you hand and foot part of the time, how about that?"

"In my day you'd have been called a Socialist."

"Would that have been a dirty word?"

"It would depend," Flora said, "on who was using it."

CHAPTER FIVE

The day that Seti Gammel came to Bramley-Wade, a week after school started, Erin had been entangled in one of her many misunderstandings. Like all the rest, it had advanced beyond the point of retreat before she actually realized that another had begun. Like the rest, it had started so harmlessly, in such a *nothing* sort of way, that she couldn't see how, once again, she'd been driven into that awful shrieking she did when perfectly simple attempts to be part of things, to get into the conversation, backfired into a kind of bear-baiting, with her playing the part of bear.

Faith Bronstein had said, when the last class before lunch finished, that she and her family were going to Switzerland at Christmas for the skiing.

She hadn't been speaking to Erin but hadn't exactly not been speaking to her either. She'd just said, to the people around her, and Erin had been on the edge of the people around her, that she'd be off to Gstaad come Christmas.

"Oh, you'll love it," Erin had said eagerly. "I mean, it's really *terrific* there."

"You've been?" Faith asked, turning her head slightly, not quite looking at Erin.

"Oh, *yes*. When we lived in—in France. We went to Switzerland lots of times. It's terrific."

"Further fascinating words from world travelers," said Fred Englund.

Erin looked at his beautiful haughty head, eyes lifted to the ceiling in the bored way he often had—his rude, bored, haughty way—and felt a familiar shriveling inside. If she'd had any sense, she thought later, if she'd had the smallest scintilla of *sense*, she'd have quit there. They didn't want to listen to her. For some reason, just about anything she said made them snicker. But foolishly she pressed on. Trying to impress them? How *asinine* can you get?

She'd said, "Oh, it's really neat in those chalets in Gstaad. At night they turn down your bed and squeeze the waist of your nighty."

At that, they all turned toward her, lips quivering, and Faith said in a stunned tone, "Did you say what I thought you said? They pinch your nighty. Pinch your nighty's *waist*?"

"Yes," Erin faltered. "They do that all over Europe, in good hotels. It's—it's awfully nice."

"Now, let's get this straight," Fred said. "They pinch your nighty when you're in it or out of it?"

"They put it on your bed at night," Erin mumbled. "It's supposed—it's supposed to be welcoming, like putting on the bedlight."

"Where do they *find* your nighty?" Rosemary Wills asked, and Carmen Edwards said, "Yes, tell us that. Do they open your *suit*cases? Now, don't go away,

Erin, we're really *interested*. I mean, *I* never heard of this before. Has anybody else heard of it?"

The circle, the Pack, which seemed to Erin to have closed around her, shook its head.

"They take your nighty," Faith said, "and never mind where they got it, Carmen—maybe in Gstaad the first thing you do when you get to your chalet, before you even piddle or look for the ski lift, is get out your nighty to be pinched. So what happens then?" she said, her eyes fixed on Erin's.

Erin looked from side to side for a way out, a way through them. She'd begun to tremble. "Let me out," she said shakily.

"No, Erin. We have to get to the bottom of this," said Fred. "It's the most interesting thing we've heard all morning. Isn't it?"

The rest of them nodded. Fred's Pack. They—Fred, Rosemary, Faith, Carmen, and Ed Kaufman, who wasn't in school that day—always said "we." As if they were royalty, or newspaper editors, Erin thought, hoping she felt scornful.

"What *I* need to know," Faith went on, "is how the *procedure* goes. I wouldn't want to make a gaffe in Gstaad, would I?" she appealed to the Pack.

"God, no," said Fred. "We want you gaffeless under all circumstances, especially in Gstaad where the *least* gaffe could trigger an avalanche. So how about it, Erin? They take your nighty—"

"Goddammit!" Erin screamed. "They take your nighty and lay it out on the bed when they turn your bed down and they pinch in its effing waist and it's supposed to look welcoming. It has something to do with *graciousness*, which is something you people wouldn't know much about. And I don't think you know much about traveling either!"

"I think," said Carmen, "if I came into a room at night and saw a nighty lying there with its waist pinched in, I'd scream. I mean, I'm sure I'd think it was a corpse. Murder in the Gstaad Guesthouse."

"What I want to know," said Fred, "is what if you don't *wear* a nighty? Personally, I sleep raw. What I want to know is, what, since I wouldn't have a nighty, would they pinch on me?" He looked around his team and added, "I hope."

This *mot* just about drowned them in laughter, and Erin, looking at Fred's handsome, happily self-satisfied face, hated him with her whole heart. None of this bunch liked her, and she never had the brains to accept that and treat them with the indifference that their rude and rotten behavior deserved, but Fred was the worst of all. Mean, stuck-up, egotistical, cruel.

She found herself screaming at him. "You pig! You turd! I'll get back at you, you just wait and see!"

"Let's go to lunch," Fred said, shrugging. "It's getting noisy here."

They went off to the dining room, leaving Erin alone in the sun-filled quiet of the classroom. There was a big wooden clock on the wall, with a brass pendulum that swung sedately, measuring moments . . . tick . . . tock . . . tick . . . tock. On sills outside the mullioned windows pigeons rambled and rumbled. Near the ceiling a wasp circled, buzzing excitedly. The only other sound was that of Erin's quick sobbing breaths.

She looked around the room, eyes blurry with rage and pain. What had it all been *about*? How could a perfectly innocent remark about Switzerland's habits of hospitality leave her like this, sick and wrung out and made a fool of once again? What was the stupid asinine girl talking about Christmas already for anyway. It wasn't even October yet. Shows how much traveling *she's* done, has to talk about a trip that's still three months off. Shows how much she—

The empty room, the clock, the pigeons, the wasp.

Maybe I should go to lunch, she thought. She wasn't hungry. If she had been hungry she could never have faced them all in the dining room. Maybe I'll go home. Yes, that was what she'd do. Go home, say she was sick. This was Friday. By Monday they'd have cooled toward her. They had a couple of other bears to bait, although she seemed to be the favorite. But Monday, by then, maybe they'd be exercising their superiority on Roby or Eloise.

She looked around the room again. The desks were in various stages of neatness and disorder. Ms. O'Neil had chrysanthemums in a copper bowl on her desk. On the blackboard were some Egyptian hieroglyphs drawn by the new boy who'd arrived this morning. They were little drawings of people's names, surrounded by bullet-shaped rectangles. Seti Gammel had explained that they were called cartouches, something Erin already knew. He'd done his own name for them, and Ms. O'Neil's, and some of the pupils', Fred Englund's among them. She didn't know how he'd picked whose name he'd do but hadn't expected him to pick hers and he hadn't. He'd done Rosemary and Faith and Fred.

Fred.

She felt a cramp, an actual physical pain, thinking about him, thinking how much she hated him. When she had first come to Bramley-Wade last year, when she had had her first sight of Fred Englund, she had nearly gasped aloud. Never in her life before had she seen anything to compare with him. Tall and blond and lithe and handsome with a smile like sun flashing on blue waters. When he was out on the basketball court, his very short shorts showing his marvelous legs, arm muscles sloping smoothly, his whole self clean and tan, he had really made her quiver. For a few weeks after that first day's inquisition, his Pack hadn't bothered with her. They'd had Roby and Eloise to torment. Last year they'd also had a young teacher, fresh out of college. They'd managed to make his life such a misery that he'd quit after Christmas and gone back to school to get a doctorate. During those blessedly peaceful weeks, Fred, every now and then, in an absent-minded way, would smile at her or address a word to her. Those brief attentions started an emotion in her, feverish and bright, like a flame licking at a log. She supposed she had fallen in love with him. Anyway, got a crush on him. Faith and Carmen and Rosemary weren't long in noticing that and they began to close in on her, and then of course they discovered how deliciously easy it was to make her lose her temper, and all peace was lost. With that, also, went any joy in Fred's presence or person, though it took longer to get over the turmoil he caused within her.

By now, nearly a year later, no trace of love sickness for him remained. She feared and disliked him, but knew something she hadn't known last year. He wasn't bright. He led his Pack by virtue of his stunning looks and the arrogance that came of looking like that and not being bright. She didn't even think he was consciously unkind, the way some of his followers were. He was cruel like a small stupid child torturing creatures smaller and more helpless than itself.

That did not make him better than the rest. It made him more terrifying.

I hate him, I hate him, she thought. He's an unspeakable turd and I'm so *tired* of having emotions about him, so tired of it—

"I'll show him," she muttered aloud and glanced toward his desk. Left his homework right out on top, he had. Just lying there, several pages of it, all written out in his neat small handwriting. It'd take him days to recreate that much work, that many words.

"I'll show him."

She stumped across the room to his desk, picked up the pages and was about to tear them to shreds when a step in the hall made her start nervously. Sheets of paper flew across the floor and Erin's eyes filled with angry tears. If it was Fred how would she explain? How would she explain no matter who it was?

Seti Gammel came into the room, smiled at Erin, and said, "Hi. Guess I got back early from lunch."

Erin looked up from her stooping position but didn't speak. Her hands shook as she tried to reassemble Fred's homework.

"Here, let me help," he said. "Are you doing your lessons during lunch hour?"

"No," Erin croaked. She cleared her throat, gave a peal of laughter that earned her a quick glance from Seti, but he just proceeded to put the papers in order and then handed them to her.

"Oh, they aren't mine," she said, laughing merrily again. "I was just picking them up for Fred. The wind—breeze—blew them off his desk." At Seti's surprised expression, she added, "I guess." There was no breeze at all. "Maybe I brushed past them," she continued miserably.

"Well, it doesn't matter, does it?" He looked around the room. "I like this school."

"I wouldn't have thought you'd been here long enough to know if you liked it or not."

"I mean I like the building. It has elegance."

"It does, doesn't it? It was somebody's old mansion, at the beginning of the century. There were lots of houses like this just off Fifth Avenue in those days. Mostly they're gone now, or turned into schools or art galleries, or else into apartments."

"This isn't what is called a 'brownstone,' is it?"

"No. This is a real mansion. Marble halls and curving staircases. Brownstones are much smaller. And narrower. We own one. A brownstone. My family, I mean. I live only a few blocks from here, off Lexington. Maybe," she said in a rush, "you'd like to come visit me, sometime. If you wanted to, that is."

He smiled pleasantly. "That would be nice. I should like to sometime."

"My father's an Egyptologist."

"He *is*?"

She ducked her head. "Not really. He'd *like* to be one. He knows as much, I bet, as most of the real ones do. My father's crazy about Egypt. Ancient, not modern, of course—" She gasped and looked at him in dismay.

Seti smiled again. He had a ready smile. It didn't come in flashing spurts, like Fred's. Seti's smile was slow and lingered in his eyes. "Ancient Egypt," he said, "is what people who want to be Egyptologists are interested in. I'm interested in it myself."

"I should think so."

"Why?"

"Well—because it's your country. You're descended from those people—the pyramid builders and all."

"Are all Americans interested in American history?"

"Probably not."

"Besides, modern Egyptians are not descended from the pyramid builders. As a people they were dispersed, extincted—no, that's not the word—made *extinct*, centuries ago. First the Greeks took over, then the Romans. Then there were years when the country was ruled over by Byzantium, and the Arabs came, and then the Turks, and then the Arabs again. The people we know as ancient Egyptians are as erased from the planet as the Etruscans are."

Oh, gosh, Erin thought sorrowfully. He's going to be too smart for me. He's so nice, and already I like him so much. Only who were the Etruscans?

"I better go," she mumbled.

"Go? Isn't there school this afternoon?"

"I—have a toothache."

"That's a shame. I hope it gets better."

"Yes, well—good-bye, Seti."

"Good-bye. It was fun talking."

He doesn't know my name, she thought, irritated with herself for being hurt. How could he know everybody's name the very first day?

She went slowly down the wide marble steps to the first floor lobby, stopped in the office, and told them she didn't feel well, although now she would probably just as soon have stayed. Talking with Seti had steadied her somehow, and probably she could have faced the Pack. Maybe. Only why should she? It was Friday afternoon and she wanted to get away from this place.

50

Mrs. Cartwright in the office was sorry about her tooth and said of course she could go home.

Out the big carved teak doors, onto Fifth Avenue. She turned to stare up at the building. It had stone gargoyles on its rather grimy facade and window boxes with geraniums flourishing in the city air. The ground floor windows were protected with curved iron grilles. The upstairs windows were mullioned and had been recently washed.

He's right, she thought. The building is elegant. At one time it had housed an elegant wealthy family. Imagine. All those rooms for one family.

Seti has elegance, she thought. The real thing. Including manners.

She blew up her cheeks, let out air with a popping noise, and started walking home.

CHAPTER SIX

Seti Gammel was taken up by Fred Englund's Pack.
He was graceful about it but didn't allow himself to
be entirely absorbed, which was probably, Erin
thought, one of the reasons they took him up. They
were accustomed to people panting to get in, and
probably he *intrigued* them, being a little bit distant,
and also Egyptian and so sort of mysterious.

There'd been some resistance to him at first by
Faith and Ed Kaufman, because they were Jews and
so had to hate an Arab. At least, that was what Faith
said. "If *he's* going to sit with us," she'd said one day
after lunch when they were all back in the classroom
except for Seti and Ms. O'Neil, "then pardon me, but
I'll eat in another corner."

"Oh, come on now," Fred said. "What's that got to
do with us, where he comes from? He's a nice guy."

"Maybe it has nothing to do with you, Fred, but *I*
am a Jew. Don't you ever read anything, or do you

think being gorgeous constitutes your whole entire role? The Jews and the Arabs hate each other."

"Yeah," said Ed. "They sure do, and if you ever read anything but *Sports Illustrated* you'd know it, Fred old boy. Those Egyptians would like to blow Israel right off the map, for your information. And we're supposed to sit down and eat with the guy? Seti Gammel. Shitty Camel is what I'd call him."

This was said as Ms. O'Neil came, walking lightly as she always did, into the room. Seti was right behind her, and Erin guessed he had to have heard. But the features of his smooth dark face remained expressionless as he went to his desk without looking at anyone.

Ms. O'Neil walked to the front of the room, smiled at them, and said, "Why don't we all sit down, and I'll tell you a story?"

Ms. O'Neil had been married and divorced. At the beginning of the year she'd explained that she preferred being referred to as Ms., since in her opinion it was one small step for humankind that no one had to be categorized by a title. Ms. O'Neil could say something like that and have it observed because she was so nice, so kind, so bright, so pretty. Erin was pretty sure that Ms. O'Neil would *not* wish to have her wishes observed because she was pretty, but a fact was a fact, even if someone in the Women's Movement didn't want to face it. Erin had heard some of the boys laughing about Women's Lib. But, to her face, they were very respectful to Ms. O'Neil. They all were.

Now they gave their attention as she leaned against the bookcase wall at the front of the room and began,

"Once upon a time there was a girl named Brefney O'Neil—"

"But that's your name," Faith interrupted. "I mean, I thought—we all thought—you'd been married."

"I was married, Faith. When I got divorced, for good and sufficient reasons, which I shall not go into, I returned to my maiden name. So—once upon a time this girl named Brefney O'Neil had a delightful father and a delightful grandfather and she loved them both very much. They had been born in Galway and were what might be called 'professional South Irishmen.' They lived in Boston—where this Brefney was born— claiming that the grandfather had a price on his head back in the *old sod* because he had fought in the Troubles with the IRA. Naturally he had a price on his head or he wouldn't have been able to hold it up.

"Now you can see that this Brefney was pretty impressionable. She found all this romantic. She *admired* her father and grandfather for their claims of violence. She learned to hate the English as they did—and that was a deal of hate for a young person to carry about. This Brefney was actually in college before she discovered that she was not obliged to loathe an Englishman on sight. That, on the contrary, she could like them and even—in one case—" Ms. O'Neil looked dreamy. "—love . . ."

There was a long pause while she looked out the window. Down the years? Erin wondered wistfully. The class waited for the end of the story with a sense of anticipation. They loved Ms. O'Neil's stories from life.

"Well," she said, coming back to them. "Where was I?"

"You were learning not to hate English people."

"You were falling in love with an English guy."

"You got the drift. So—Brefney O'Neil spent a good part of her youth supporting this hatred in her system. It did her great harm. Hatred is a debilitating, degenerating, debasing emotion. It warps, wastes. And there is an interesting thing about hatred—it must be taught. It is not an automatic response that comes with us at birth, like the fear of falling, say. We have to be taught to hate, and this Brefney was systematically, deliberately taught to hate. Not a country, and a history of wrongs, and there *were* wrongs done. She was taught to hate people, individuals. A whole nation of them. She came to her senses in time to realize that she'd been drugged, in time to try corrective measures. But the truth is you can never entirely eradicate seeds sown so early. It's like witch grass. You can think you've pulled it up entirely, cleared your garden forever, but always one day, among the flowers, you will find the ugly roots of the witch grass taking hold again. And I do believe that's the end of my story. Shall we open our history books to page 123 and begin?"

There was speculation afterward about Ms. O'Neil's story. The favorite theory was that she'd fallen in love with an Englishman and married him and then the marriage had gone bad because of what her father and grandfather had taught her. Probably *they* had cast her out of their lives, and after all those years of thralldom she could not bear to be without their love, so she turned against her English husband, and the witch grass had taken hold in the garden of their love, and now Ms. O'Neil was back to her maiden name and—if you could go by how she behaved—lonely for her lost Englishman. *Dear Enemy*, Erin thought.

Wasn't there a book by that title? He, her husband, had been her dear enemy. Well, it was awful and a shame, and she was right about hating. Erin decided not to hate Fred Englund or his rat pack anymore. Because it was bad for her. Because Ms. O'Neil said it was bad to hate, and she believed anything Ms. O'Neil said.

And Seti was gradually, though not—by his own choice—entirely, taken into the Pack because of what Ms. O'Neil had said. Well, not entirely that, either. Seti just was so nice. He was not, as Ed Kaufman pointed out, Egypt. He was just this great guy who happened to *come* from Egypt. His father was something high-up at the United Nations, and there they were trying to get nations and people to understand one another. No, it'd be wrong and dumb, they said, to take out international distrusts and suspicions, international hatreds, on one guy going to school with them. Especially when the guy was Seti.

Erin didn't have confidants at school. She didn't have friends. Except for Fred and his gang, nobody paid much attention to her unless she was having a temper tantrum, when the Pack closed in more tightly, fascinated by her lack of control, and all else backed off more conspicuously.

So she made a confidante of Flora. The only person whose attention she could really get and hold was her father, but during his frequent absences, Flora was *there*, and she listened and, Erin felt, did care, even if she had this habit of interrupting with remarks not at all to Erin's point. Erin could be telling about a dream (she loved to tell her dreams, which were interesting and unusual) and Flora would appear to be paying

56

attention. Then all at once she'd say something like, "I do believe I'll put barley in the soup. Your father doesn't care for barley, but the soup'll be used up by the time he's back." Deflated, Erin would refuse to continue with her dream, unless considerably coaxed by Flora, *after* she'd put the barley in the soup.

"I think," she said, having told Flora of Ms. O'Neil's story, "that she's probably the best teacher I'll have in my whole life. I think I'll always remember her and the wise things she says."

"Well, *I* think," Flora muttered, "that if she's such a much as you go on about, she might—"

"Might what?" Erin said in a cold tone when Flora fell abruptly silent.

"Nothing."

"Might *what*? Are you *criticizing* Ms. O'Neil?"

"I only meant," Flora burst out, "that if she's such a fine teacher and all why doesn't she pay more attention to the people who need—attention paid to them? That's all I was saying."

"Well, it's enough," Erin said angrily. "You don't know her, so you have no right to say anything. She's *busy*. And she can't pay attention to *everything*."

"Okay, okay," said Flora, growing heated in turn. "So you've got a crush on the teacher and she can do no wrong—"

"Don't you dare!" Erin got to her feet, shaking. "You—you witch. Don't you say such a thing about me!"

"Oh, come off it, Erin. All kids get a crush on their teacher. It's like fractions—just comes along at a certain period and then it's time for the next subject. Don't get in such a lather."

But Erin slammed out of the kitchen and up the

back stairs to her room, where she lay on the bed, shaking with tears and trying not to hate Flora, too. The way things were going, she'd drown in the—the *ichor* of hate. But why did dumb Flora have to say such a dumb thing? Not about having a crush—because maybe I do or maybe I don't, Erin thought. She wasn't exactly sure and didn't exactly care. She'd only pretended to get angry at that because what had made the rage and panic rise within her was what Flora had said first. Why didn't Ms. O'Neil pay attention to people who needed attention paid to them? Why doesn't she ever pay any attention to *me*—never notice that I need *help*?

Awful, horrible Flora, putting her plump finger on horrible, awful truths. Ms. O'Neil paid attention to winners. To attractive people, to secure people. She'd told a marvelous story—Flora had called it a homily— and maybe in the telling actually had helped save some people from the awful fate of hating. Anyway, she'd helped Seti over a tough spot.

But Ms. O'Neil—Ms. O'Neil was not—she was not the person Erin had thought she was, wanted her to be. Not the best and wisest teacher she'd ever know. Ms. O'Neil was a nice enough, bright and pretty person, who was kind to bright nice pretty people.

And I never even noticed, never *really* noticed, Erin thought, turning onto her back, elbow across her eyes, tears trickling to a stop. I never took it in until Flora pointed it out.

I'm stupid. Not only do I look like I look, with this awful kinky hair that I can't do anything about and this body that isn't at all like a wand—everybody goes around calling *her* a wand—and this nothing collection of eyes and nose and so forth on this nothing sort of head. All that—and stupid, too. *She* would say I was feeling sorry for myself, but darn it all, I'm somebody that *somebody* ought to feel sorry for.

She stopped crying and squeezed her arms together across her chest, trying to ward off an impending sensation so bad that it made tears irrelevant. It came at her this way. No warning. She became anxious, hideously anxious. Frightened. "Oh, don't," she moaned, as the familiar, the awful feeling seeped through her body, gradually, steadily, so that after a few moments she felt bloated by it. She could feel her heart beat. It slapped around like a Ping-Pong ball in her sadly undeveloped chest. Trying to analyze, to be cool, to reason the horror away, she felt her body swell until her skin felt tight. She looked at her fingers. They felt to her like frankfurters, though they retained their usual thin shape. Her head hummed and seemed to roll about. She wanted to get up and start running, running—but lay as if nailed to the bed.

What *is* this, what is it? she wondered. *What is this feeling and why does it come?* Why doesn't it go away? It will go away. It always goes away. Why doesn't it go away sooner? Why does it happen at all?

Think about something, now. *Think about something.* Posey. Think about her. How do you suppose Posey is doing in Greenwich, Connecticut, in Aunt Marthe's gleaming house? Does she pick at the upholstery there? No, she doesn't have to because she's allowed to go outside where she can claw at trees. How's it with you, Posey, my little companion? Missing me? What it is about cats—they're so calm. Not placid. Calm. Cool. *They* don't suffer from anxiety, oh, no. They aren't like people. Not like dogs, either. I think dogs get anxious. They're always running, running, as if they knew where they were going and were already late. Cats never run. Unless from danger. Cats know there's nowhere to go—

She might have asked the doctor about this feeling the last time she'd been in his office for a check-up, only she couldn't get over another feeling she'd been having at the time—that the doctor was more interested in the mother than in the patient. Wrong, of course. Undoubtedly wrong. He's a good doctor and knows his business and he would have fixed his nice kind eyes on mine and said—something helpful. Still, she hadn't asked him and probably never would.

At last, at last, it was subsiding. Leaving her weak, a little ashamed. Not that it was anything to be *ashamed* of, probably. Well. Just the same, it was going. It never did last long, only seemed unending while it went on—

She flung her arm across her forehead. Her hair was damp. She sat up and pulled a soft throw over herself, pulling it all around her until there was just room to breathe.

There were things to be afraid of in life. Plenty of things. Like—like something might happen to her father. That was terrifying. That was the worst. All that flying around in airplanes he did. And she couldn't live if anything happened to him. That was the worst. So bad that even while she was afraid for him she couldn't believe anything could ever *really* happen to him. But there were other things, and all of them real enough. Danger on the streets. An accident that might leave you blind, so you couldn't read. Crippled, so you couldn't walk. Perverts. Somebody showing you something hideous and disgusting. That had happened to Carmen once. She'd told everybody about it for days not, for once, as if she were trying to be the center of attention, but as if it had been so ghastly that she was trying to share it out and maybe in that way thin the memory.

Plenty of things to be afraid of that you *knew* about.

Was it worse to be afraid of something you couldn't identify? *This* afraid? Or did it only feel that way while you were feeling it?

I wish I had a cat, she thought. Even Posey, who was not the smartest animal in the world, had been a very good listener.

CHAPTER SEVEN

"I have to go to Atlanta tomorrow," Mr. Gandy said at dinner.

"You do, dear? Why?"

"The factory we use down there has been struck. The men walked out this morning. I have to find some other source of supply we can use till this thing is settled. Maybe Richmond could give us more. I don't see how they can double their supply, though."

"I don't think people should be allowed to strike. Darling, *don't* look so dismayed when I say things. After all, think it *through*. Do the men in any particular union give a hoot about the men in another union? The miners strike and everyone everywhere suffers, but do *they* care? The rest of us could starve or freeze—just so *they* get *their* wage hikes and extra holidays and whatall. And the same goes for *all* unions. The good of them*selves*, that's all they're interested in."

"Suppose *you* think it through, Belle. Countries

where workers are not allowed to strike are called totalitarian. They *are* totalitarian. And I wouldn't want—"

"I didn't say there couldn't be arbitration, did I? Compulsory arbitration, where everybody stayed *on* the job while whatever they're fussing about got settled *for* them."

"That still does not come out to people's being able to strike, on their own, for what they feel are valid reasons. In countries where your kind of arbitration is used, it's enforced by bayonets."

"Well, that *sounds* fine, but the unions are going to strike us back to the Stone Age. Look at Italy. Don't tell me the unions there, and in England, and in this country don't abuse their right to strike."

"They're shortsighted. No more than management. Everybody takes the short-term view."

"Greedy. Greedy, greedy, greedy."

"Being greedy and shortsighted is not the prerogative of labor. It's the God-given gift of politicians and voters and workers and employers and parents and children. And so forth. To be shortsighted is human. To overcome the consequences by force is tyranny. I'd rather go back to the Stone Age than be tyrannized over. But I have to go to Atlanta first."

"Oh, Daddy!" Erin shrieked. "Oh, you're so *funny*! You say such awfully funny *things*."

"Lamb," said Mrs. Gandy, talking almost but not quite through her teeth. "Sweetie, *can't* you do something about that laugh? I remind you and remind you that it just is not at*trac*tive to burst into—into *hoots*. Half the time what you're laughing at isn't even funny, is it, Peter?"

"*I* thought I was rather witty," he mumbled.

Erin fixed on him a look of sad courage—a look she

could summon at will and which she knew clutched painfully at his heart. Even as she assumed the expression, both meaning and exaggerating it, she thought to herself, *poor Daddy.*

Belle contemplated her daughter for a moment, turned her attention back to her husband. "When do we go?"

"I'm going alone. It'll be a quick trip and all business. I don't want to be—distracted," he said, attempting to sound playful, and failing.

"I won't distract you, I *promise*. I won't get in your way the least bit. I'll shop. Or visit Helen Stewart. She still lives in Atlanta, you know. Even after the divorce—"

"Belle, I'm going alone."

"Well. Well, of course I can't *thrust* myself on you. If you don't *want* me—"

"You know it isn't that. Oh, blast—"

For a while they continued the meal in silence. Mrs. Gandy's dark, heavily lashed eyes remained fixed on her husband with hurt attention. She moved her plate delicately from her. Peter Gandy continued to eat, clearly without savor. Erin chewed and watched them.

She'll talk him around. She won't even have to talk. She'll just *look* him around. He wanted to say something to her just then. He wanted to ask her to stop picking at me. But he never would. Not, anyway, unless they were alone. If he ever said anything to her at those times Erin didn't know. Not that it would make any difference.

The silence lengthened. It stretched.

"There's a new boy at school," Erin said loudly.

"He's Egyptian. His father is ambassador to the United Nations."

"Egyptian?"

"Ambassador?"

"Well—anyway, somebody important. Maybe not ambassador."

Mrs. Gandy subsided, but Peter Gandy's attention was caught.

"What's he like?"

"Nice. Even if—awfully nice." She'd never mentioned her problems with Fred's Pack to her parents. After France she'd never mentioned any school problems to them. "I told him about *Antony and Cleopatra,* Daddy. He's seen it, too. Cleopatra was a Ptolemy. She came along very late, when Egypt wasn't really a great or independent nation anymore."

"I told you that."

"I know. I remember you did. Seti told me, too. That's his name. Seti Gammel. He likes very ancient history, too. Egyptian. Back around Tuthmosis and pharaohs like him. Thousands of years ago. He says modern Egyptians aren't descended from the pharaohs at all."

"That's right. They share a particular area of the planet, the Nile Valley, but they don't have anything else in common. Actually, Egypt is more properly called the United Arab Republic."

"That's what Seti says. That's what they call it at the United Nations, he says."

"Haven't you ever been to the United Nations, Erin?"

"Flora and I went over once. But nothing was in *session.* We just looked in the rooms. Daddy, who were the Etruscans?"

"A nation of—"

"Peter, *please*. Flora's waiting to serve dessert. *If* we're going to this concert, you'd better let her serve it."

"Sorry. Okay, Flora, bring it on. Too bad you can't come with us tonight, Erin. Julius Rudel conducting Bach and Mozart—"

"She'd be bored to death."

"No, I wouldn't. I mean, how do I know if—"

"It's a school night. You have work to do."

"No, I don't. I—"

"Erin. Love. Please. Don't pester. Anyway, aren't you going to wash your hair tonight? It must need it. When did you last shampoo it?"

Erin squirmed. She hated her hair, washed or unwashed. Hated to look at it, feel it. It seemed that all the other girls at Bramley-Wade, even fat Claudia, had this hair that fell in shimmering waterfalls, perhaps waving ever so slightly, but usually straight and gleaming as curtains. Her own, dark and without lustre, reminded her of corrugated packing material. Left to itself, it usually fell around her head like a lampshade. Pulled back in a ponytail, with those bangs practically touching her eyebrows, she looked about thirty years old, but that at least kept it from sticking out.

"Couldn't we get it straightened again?" she asked.

"We've tried that twice. Your hair just isn't the kind that will straighten properly. I know what you *want* it to look like, but you might as well accept the fact that it never will. You should do what Pepe suggested, cut it short. He's an expert barber and could probably make you look quite *cute*."

"Nobody wears short hair. I'd look *silly*."

"Well, you admit yourself that the way it is *now—*"

"Belle! Don't talk to her that way. Please. I know you don't mean to—"

"Darling man, I mean what I mean. It isn't going to do Erin any good for us to *avoid* matters. Now, her hair is a problem, but it's a problem we should try to *meet*. Now, Pepe says—"

Mr. Gandy got to his feet. "I don't want any dessert. I'll be in the den when you're ready, Belle."

"Oh, for the *love* of heaven. What a way to start an evening out." Throwing a reproachful glance at Erin, Mrs. Gandy went in a graceful rush after her husband.

Flora, who'd been fussing at the sideboard, said, "Want yours, honey? It's floating island, just the way you like it."

Elbow on the table, chin in one palm, Erin stared through the dining-room door at the table in the hallway where a porcelain bowl of flowers was reflected in the mirror. Pretty.

Flora put a dish of custard and a few sugar wafers in front of her. "Eat it, Erin. It's delicious, if I do say so."

Erin picked up her spoon and gulped. "Delicious."

"Tell you what—after they're gone, if you'll help in the kitchen, I'll help with your hair. Okay?"

"That'd be nice."

In the morning, at breakfast, Mrs. Gandy said, "Erin, it really is such an unfortunate habit you have, that of sulking. You didn't even say good-*bye* to us last night. Was that nice?"

"You didn't say good-bye to me, either."

"Because we were in a hurry—"

"I'm sorry about that, Erin," Mr. Gandy said. "We

67

got out of here in such a thrash that I didn't think till we were well on our way."

"How was the concert, Daddy?"

"Glorious. I listened to the Mozart—*The Abduction From the Seraglio*—and thought, now if I flew straight up to the gates of heaven and went right on through and somebody asked what I was doing there, I'd just reply, 'I came up on a contrabassoon, but it's all right, I'll be leaving presently.' Because, of course, you always have to leave."

"Erin, I thought you were going to wash your hair."

Erin took a deep breath. She looked at the woman across the table. Black feathered curls. Short. Long neck. Long and lustrous eyes. She catalogued coldly for a moment before saying, "I did wash it. You can check with Flora, if you want. What you see before you is a *washed* head of hair."

But then—joy, joy!—they telephoned from Mr. Gandy's office and said the strike in Atlanta had been settled after an all-night bargaining session. So, since he had the day off but now did not need to make the trip, he and Erin took their bicycles over to the park and rode for a couple of hours and had lunch at a hot dog vendor's.

Bliss, bliss!

CHAPTER EIGHT

"Hey, Seti," said Fred Englund on Friday afternoon, "now hear this. We've got this great idea. We're gonna make a movie. I got a camera for my birthday. Zoom lens and everything. We'll work out the details as we go, but my idea is we make this film switching back and forth between modern days and ancient Egypt. We can maybe use the Metropolitan Museum, film some stuff in there, we'll have to find out, but anyway you're going to be Rameses II. We can make it real spooky. We're going to make sets in the shop here and shoot some stuff on location, and it'll be a ball, right?"

Seti smiled. "Rameses II is not my favorite pharaoh. There actually were some not so—so overweening."

"Okay, old buddy. Pick your pharaoh and give us the dirt on his times."

"Don't you think you'd better do a little research yourself? Wouldn't that be better than if—"

"Oh, sure, sure. We're going to. But we gotta take

advantage of the swell weather to do our outdoor shooting. Want to get Cleopatra's Needle in, that's over in Central Park."

"That obelisk, you know, has nothing to do with Cleopatra. It's inscribed with the cartouche of Tuthmosis III. He was a couple of thousand years before Cleopatra."

"Well, it's still as Egyptian as you can get, isn't it? So okay. We'll shot outdoors as much as we can, and then in the museum, and *then* read some history. Right? How about it, Seti?"

"Erin here," Seti said, "is really the most Egyptian looking of all of us. Except for maybe me, that is."

Erin, who'd been gathering her books, not paying much attention, looked up at the sound of her name.

Fred and Erin looked at each other blankly.

"Don't you see it?" Seti pursued. "The ancient Egyptians were sort of short, with long dark eyes like Erin's and the same marvelous long necks. Even her hair, if she didn't pull it back, has the look of women in the temple and tomb paintings. She looks like one of the daughters of Amenhotep III."

Erin listened in astonishment. That was how she often thought of *her* as looking. Only on *her,* a long neck and long eyes came out to Nefertiti. On me, Erin thought harshly, it comes out to a camel. Both as Egyptian as you can get, of course.

"Definitely, we should have Erin in our movie," Seti said.

Erin's face flushed and she felt her palms grow slippery.

"Great idea," said Fred. "I haven't exactly got a role for her yet, but we'll work her in all right. What say, Erin?"

Erin gulped and nodded. "That'd—I'd—yes, I'd like—"

"Swell. I'll let you know when we're ready for you, okay?"

Erin nodded. He sounded like a movie producer already. Don't call me, I'll call you. She smiled painfully at Seti, ducked her head, and hurried from the room.

That evening, sitting in the den, looking at the television news while she waited for Flora to call her for dinner, she thought about Fred as a movie producer and wondered what he'd do when he found out, as she was pretty sure he would, that they wouldn't let him make his epic in the Metropolitan. They practically didn't let you carry anything in, except a purse. There was a checkroom where umbrellas, parcels, briefcases, all things like that, had to be stashed so nobody would go sticking their ferrule through a Rembrandt, tucking a tiny Monet in a folder, or planting a bomb in the Egyptian mastaba.

Well, he'd find out.

On the TV screen, a woman was interviewing a young musician. She'd missed his name. A beautiful black young man with a guitar that he strummed softly as he spoke.

"Well, I've made it," he was saying. "Sort of accidentally, you might say, but here I am. On top. Golden record and all, so I guess this is the top, all right."

"But you must have worked very hard to get where you are," said the interviewer.

"Oh, sure. Count on that. Worked my—worked like a demon all my life. But *making* it. That was an accident."

"You write your own music and lyrics, don't you?"

"Yeah. I tried singing other folks' stuff, but it—

didn't grab me the right way. I've always had to—to work from inside out. And *inside,* that's where my own music is, okay? You gotta understand—I been lonely all my life. Maybe not now so much, or maybe just as much but there's so many people around I don't notice anymore. But up till—oh, say twenty minutes ago, twenty months ago—whenever all this started, I was lonely, lonely, lonely—and it's my *theory* that if you're lonely you become creative because you just can't sit there saying, 'Man, nothin's anywhere, so I won't think.' You gotta *think.* You think things. You dream. You maybe cre*ate* something out of your dreams, okay? I mean, I think that all people who write something—books, music, anything—they do it from being lonely. At least, that's my opinion."

Erin stared at him. He looked, sounded, too honest, too *pure,* to be making all that up. Just for an effect. It'd be the worst kind of a lie to say something like that and not mean it. But how could somebody so really beautiful be lonely? He wore a gorgeous embroidered shirt and a chain of gold beads. His smooth dark face was beautiful, beautiful. There just wasn't a different word. He was talented, too, that was plain. Wrote his own music and lyrics, had had a golden record made. How could *he* be lonely? How could he ever have been? In school he'd have been just as breathtaking and probably had showed musical talent very early. So how could he—

She leaned forward, anxious to catch his name. Maybe she'd write him a letter and ask—

"Erin. Erin. Dinner's ready!"

Flora's voice interrupted the interviewer's, and the scene on the screen switched to an advertisement. Oh, well, Erin thought, going into the kitchen to eat with

Flora. Oh, well—I wouldn't have written to him anyway, probably. If I really wanted to write, I could call the TV station and find out who he was. But probably I'd write and he wouldn't answer anyway.

"They just had the nicest young man on the TV. Plays an electric guitar."

She never said what she meant. Almost never said what she meant. Maybe once in a while to her father. But suppose she said to Flora, "I just saw an angel, and I'll never forget him all my life. He said words that moved into my heart and will be there forever, and it's almost a privilege to be lonely if it's a feeling *he's* known, too. And I think I'm in love with him, but anyway I love him and I always will."

Flora would shake her head. "How you go on," she'd say.

It's true, just the same. I love him and I'll always love him.

"Must you be so histri*onic?*" said a voice in her mind. "This is all so ex*cess*ive."

"Well, if I just do it in my own head," Erin replied defiantly, "I can be as histri*onic* as I want to be."

"Electric guitars," Flora was saying. "Electric toothbrushes, electric swizzle sticks. Nobody does anything by hand anymore."

"But an electric guitar isn't the same as those others."

"They're all the same to me," Flora said. "Bone lazy, just about the whole world. That's why there's so many divorces."

"Because of electric toothbrushes?"

"Don't come over me with that, Missy. You're smart enough to know what I mean. Because everything comes too easy. People don't have enough to occupy themselves with, everything being done for them by Con Ed. Leaves too much time to get into trouble, too much time to think about themselves when they should be thinking about other people, thinking about getting ahead."

"That's not the same thing, is it? Thinking about other people and thinking about getting ahead?"

"You can think about more than one thing at a time. You can do a little good in the world and do a little good for yourself, too. But no—all these young people, they've copped out. Gone off to eat alfalfa and spin wool in the woods."

"But that's not using electric toothbrushes, Flora. That's doing things by *hand.*"

"Miss Contrary, that's you."

Erin didn't think she was the contrary one. "The pot roast's good, Flora. Marvelous."

"My own recipe. Made with beer and aged several days to bring all the flavor out, and then they go to some restaurant and pay a fortune for something that was probably frozen last summer. And the service! I *guess* that's what they call it, though I'd blush to say aloud what *I'd* call it. The surliest people you'll find in this city are waiters in so-called good restaurants. Your father and mother took me to one of these places for my birthday where you need to make a reservation like it was elective surgery and it was a shame and a disgrace the way those waiters did their job, slapping the food down in front of a person like putting a dish down for the dog. Plates too hot, food practically cold, and I bet the whole thing set your father back a hundred dollars, easy. No, don't talk to me about people doing their jobs, young lady. Now, what would you say to a homemade éclair?"

"I'd say *bon appétit!*"

She went to bed before her parents got in. Probably they'd gone to the theatre or something, she hadn't really listened when *she* said.

It was a warm fall night, windows open, curtains lifting gently into the room. Erin looked around, knowing it was a pretty room. She was a fortunate person. After all, what more could she ask than what she had? Well, she'd ask for a cat, given the chance. She missed Posey's bland, beautiful presence. It had been nice having Posey curled up beside her on the bed while she read. Nice to have Posey to talk to.

You can't just sit there saying nothing's going on, so I won't think. You gotta think, and maybe dream, and out of dreaming maybe you create—

Was that how he'd put it? Close enough. With a sigh, she picked up *Jane Eyre,* knocking *Alice* to the floor. Well, anyway, she was through with that. *Through the Looking Glass* had been a little better, just as acid but anyhow more interesting, than *Alice.* The beginning, with the conversations with Dinah and the black kitten, the snow outside, and the fire— all that had been cozy and pleasant. And going through the mirror. That part was marvelous. Boy, would *I like* to go through a mirror, Erin thought. Through a glass, into another world—

CHAPTER NINE

"Okay, everybody," Fred said. "We're going to have a story conference during study period. Ms. O'Neil says okay to that and I've asked her to sit in, as a sort of adviser *ex cathedra*."

"What does that mean, Chief?"

"Oh, *ex cathedra*, you know what that means. It's an expression that's used all the time."

"In cinema circles?"

"I don't know in what circles. It just means she's the teacher and it's polite to ask her to sit in on our conference, okay?"

"Okay with me. I just don't think you know what you're talking about."

"All right, all right," said Fred. "Let's get the show on the road. Oh, here you are, Ms. O'Neil—now, do you want to sit at your desk or in the circle here with the company?" He thought that over and added, "The troupe."

Ms. O'Neil, clearly struggling not to laugh, said

she'd be glad to sit with the company if that was all right with everybody. "It's your project, and I don't want to interfere in anyway."

She had, and the entire class knew it, already interfered to the point of persuading Fred to make it a class venture and not just a romp for him and his gang. How she'd done this, since it was Fred's camera after all, Erin couldn't think, but imagined she'd partly wheedled and partly put it that if he insisted on making it exclusive they wouldn't be able to use the school for costume making, story conferences, etc.

Story conference, indeed, thought Erin, remembering how once she'd fluttered at the sight of beautiful, masterful, casually unkind Fred. Now he put her in mind of Humpty Dumpty. Huffing and puffing. Putting on airs.

"Okay," said Fred, when they were all seated on the floor, having pushed chairs and desks against the wall. "Okay, now the first thing is to get some idea of what we're going to do."

"No flies on Fred," said Ed Kaufman. He was rewarded with a sputter of laughter.

Fred gave him a quick, impatient glance but did not take offense. Fred, Erin said to herself, doesn't take offense at anything because he can't imagine anyone's being in a position to offend him. So far as Fred was concerned, someone attempting to put him down would be the flea on the lion's lip.

Imagine being that sure of yourself, she mused. *Imagine*.

"Since I'm the director of this film," Fred went on, "I'll—"

"Why should you be the director?" Roby asked

bravely. The Pack surveyed him with surprise, then looked to Fred for his response.

"It's my camera," he said gently. "And my idea. Okay? Okay. Any more questions like that before we get down to business?"

There were none.

"We're going to do this movie about somebody being transported back to ancient Egypt."

"Did you find out if they'll let us film stuff in the Metropolitan?"

"No, but—"

"Don't you think you ought to do that first, huh?"

"No. We'll work up our story line and have something to show them. They'll probably fall all over themselves. Give their old museum a little publicity."

Erin's eye accidentally caught Seti's. He gave her a slow smile. Warming. Pleasing.

"What we'll do," Fred said, "is we'll start with this mummy—what are you smiling at, Seti?"

"It wasn't anything, really, Fred. I just—had a bet with myself. I bet you'd start with a mummy and you did, that's all."

"Well, what else do you start with in ancient Egypt? Christ, the place was crawling with mummies. Oh, sorry, Ms. O'Neil. Slip of the tongue."

"Which one?" she asked.

"Huh? Oh—oh, hey—here, Seti, I didn't mean anything by that. Mean to say, old buddy, I'm sure there were plenty of other things your ancestors did besides wrap up their bodies in bandages—"

"Fred," said Seti. "Would you mind if I spoke slurringly about the Onondaga Indians?"

"Onondaga *Indians*? Why should I mind what you say about them?"

"They're as much your ancestors as the ancient Egyptians are mine. But you're right, they did do more than wrap themselves up in bandages. They had a very rich and complicated civilization when the rest of the world was still running around in skins and grunting."

"From what I've heard, all they ever did was get ready to shove off."

Seti sighed. "That's because they built their tombs and temples of materials that last, so that's what you see today. Tombs and temples. But if you pay attention to what's in them—to the furniture and jewelry and beautiful dishes and things in the tombs, if you look at the wall paintings in the tombs and temples and see the sort of life they show, or read the hieroglyphics and understood what they say—then you just have to come up with a very lively, life-loving race. They planned to pick up right where they left off when they died, except everything would be better. Nobody would suffer, or get old, or have toothaches or diseases. Have you been to the Metropolitan and seen some of the things that have been found in the tombs?" he asked Fred.

"Yeah. I went over the other day and took a look. Pretty neat, some of it. Those boats they had. Really cool. And the little wooden figures of people working while the important guy lolls around. Yeah, I liked it."

"Those are Sun Boats. They carried the dead man, who was called an Osiris, not a mummy—because when a man died, he not only got judged by the god of death and birth, Osiris, in a way he *became* Osiris. They carried him through the river of night so that he could rise in the morning with Re. Re was the supreme deity, the Sun, And the little figures—those are

79

called shabti. The Egyptians were very democratic about the next world. Anyone could get there if he passed the judgment of Osiris and his Court. And *anyone*—even including Pharaoh—could be commanded to work. Real manual labor, like plowing and rowing and grinding corn. Of course the important men had no intention of working in the next world because that wouldn't make it an improvement on *this* world, so they had these shabti images put in their tombs, inscribed with orders. The inscription usually said, 'O, this shabti! If thy master is required for any labor, say thou: "Here am I." ' And then the shabti would go and hoe the ground or herd the cattle—or whatever."

"Neat," said Rosemary. "That's for me. A couple of shabtis—in this world, for a preference. They wouldn't even have to herd cattle. Just take care of *me*."

Seti smiled. "Where he couldn't take everything in its actual form," he continued enthusiastically, "a man would have representations painted on the wall of his tomb. A thousand loaves of bread and a thousand casks of beer and five hundred or so of wine, and so forth—"

"Drinkers, eh?" Fred interrupted. "We'll have a drunk scene." When Seti opened his mouth with the clear intention of continuing his history lesson, Fred added hastily, "That was great, Seti. Very informative. But let's use the rest of the time knocking this script together—"

"What script?" said Ed.

Fred looked at him in exasperation. "You don't know how movie people work, old buddy. They just sit tossing an idea around till it takes off. All right? Try it on the dog, as we say in show biz."

"That's what we say?" Faith asked happily.

80

"If we know what we're talking about we do."

"But *do* we, that's the point," said Ed.

"We'll come as close as we can, okay? Now, Seti here doesn't want to start with a mummy."

"I didn't say that. All I said is I was sure *you'd* start with one."

"So, what'll we start with instead?"

Silence.

"Well, how about it, Seti?" Fred said impatiently. "You're the expert."

Seti shrugged. "You might start at the Court of Osiris, with the dead man being judged—"

"You mean don't have somebody transported back to ancient times, just start there?"

"You could. Or—you know, the ancient Egyptians were a very conservative people and hated to give up an idea once they'd got it. That's the reason for so many gods. They never abandoned a belief or a god, they just added more as they went along. And with a civilization that lasted about four thousand years, some contradictions just had to creep in. The thing is, Egyptians didn't mind contradictions at all. They just went ahead and believed everything at once, so besides believing that the dead went to the Isles of Bliss, or the Fields of Favor, or the West—there were lots of names for the next world—they also believed that after death a person could start way down on the scale of creation and work his way up—if that's the word for it—to being human again. He could start as an insect, say, and go along to being a hoopoe bird, and then a hippopotamus, and then through superior animals like lions or leopards and so into his skin again, and it all took about three thousand years."

Well, why not, thought Erin. People have believed

81

all sorts of things. They've believed in heaven, in hell, in the stars, in nothing at all. Why not believe in coming full circle after three thousand years?

"Anyway, there's that idea. You might work it in somehow, so as to have your man starting back there and coming up to these times—"

"Must it," Ms. O'Neil said, "always be a man, Seti? You've used the masculine pronoun throughout this dissertation."

Seti gave her his inscrutable look. "Sorry, Ms. O'Neil."

"From what I've read," she said, "the women of ancient Egypt were quite emancipated. In fact, the throne and the wealth descended through the female line, not from father to son."

Seti nodded. "Except it was always a man who actually sat on the throne and was considered to be the god. The God-King had to marry to *get* there, all right, but the queen didn't sit there. He did."

"Except for Hatshepsut," said Ms. O'Neil.

"And she always dressed like a man."

The class followed this exchange, its taut undertones, with interest and was disappointed to find that Seti and Ms. O'Neil were not going to square off after all. They looked at each other for a moment and then Ms. O'Neil glanced at Fred. "Back to you," she said.

"Huh? Yeah, okay. Well, let's break and take ten."

Faith and Rosemary giggled. "Fred, you're too much," Rosemary said. "Take ten. Fancy that."

Fred grinned. "I'm not going to have a story conference and miss the chance to say 'take ten.'"

"It's more like 'take twenty-four,'" said Ed Kaufman. "Hours, I mean. The period's over, and I'm due at basketball practice."

They broke up, scattered, and Erin, going downstairs and out to the street, wondered if the whole idea was a put-on and pastime for Fred, so he could call story conferences and say "take ten" and then start playing with some other idea. He doesn't, she thought, have an awfully long attention span.

And once he'd seemed so riveting.

"Hello, Erin."

She turned, and her heart skipped. "Where did you come from, Seti?"

"Same place you did."

"Oh, how dumb of me. I mean, how did you—I—" She stopped before she could flounder into deeper, dumber waters. Seti fell into step beside her.

"Going home?"

Erin nodded.

"I'll walk with you for a while okay?"

"That'd be swell."

They walked to Madison, across Park Avenue, uptown a couple of blocks, and turned east again, reaching Erin's house without another word being spoken. It wasn't, Erin realized, a nervous silence. They were just walking along together, not talking, like a couple of people who'd known each other for a long time and for the moment felt no need to speak.

When they got to her house, Seti looked up at the narrow old brownstone building with its flourishing window boxes and nodded. "Nice."

"Seti—would you come in? For cocoa or something?" she said breathlessly.

"I'd like that."

They mounted the steps, Erin getting out her keys, hoping her hand wouldn't shake. Where a few minutes before she'd felt calm enough, now she was nervously elated.

The door opened and Flora was there, with her string marketing bag.

"Oh. It's you. Why didn't you ring, Erin?"

"I have my key," she said. Gasped? "Flora, this is Seti Gammel, he's from school. This is our friend, Flora Todd."

"Housekeeper," said Flora.

"Does that mean not friend?" Erin said sharply. "Anyway, we're going to make some cocoa."

Flora turned back into the house. "I'll do it."

"No, that's okay. You can go marketing."

"I'm delighted to stay and make cocoa," Flora said firmly. "You two go in the living room and have fun. I mean, go in and talk."

Seti and Erin looked at each other when Flora had gone down the hall to the kitchen.

What'll he *think*, Erin wondered painfully. He'll think she doesn't want to leave us alone. He'll think she thinks we'll—*do* something.

Seti grinned. "Shall we go in and have fun?"

Face flaming, Erin led the way to the living room, almost wishing she hadn't asked him. Awful Flora. You could spoil a thing for somebody, behaving the way Flora had. Defiantly, she pushed back the damper in the hearth and touched a match to the laid fire. That would mean either keeping it going till her mother got home, or not having a fire this evening at all, or laying another one on the hot ashes. Probably *she* would be irked, since she wanted a fire every evening from October to May.

"How nice that is," Seti said. "We live in this apartment on the nineteenth floor, over there by the

United Nations. They don't have fireplaces. And of course we don't have them in Egypt. I think this is only the third fire I've ever seen—in a fireplace. Why do you do that?"

"Do what?" she said.

"Blow up your cheeks that way."

"Oh, golly. I don't know. It feels good, I guess," she muttered. Her eyes widened because all at once Seti's cheeks were ballooning out, first one, then the other, then both together. He popped the air out and said, "Hey, you know, it does feel sort of good. I've noticed you doing that in school, but I never thought to try it before."

"Well, it looks simply awful."

"Doesn't it, though?" Seti filled his cheeks again, swished air about in his mouth, blew it out, laughing. "Ooof. Exercise for the face. Our poor faces, come to think of it, don't get much exercise."

He's the nicest person, Erin thought. Just the nicest person. Maybe, at that, she could look on her *mannerism* as exercise and in that case do it in the morning, in the privacy of her room, like deep breathing or push-ups. Not that she'd even been able to do a push-up. But exercising in private—that would make sense. And it might just turn out that she'd quit making faces at school. It was worth trying.

"You've started the fire," Flora said, coming in with a tea tray. "How nice."

Erin looked at her suspiciously, but the plain round face was innocent of anything but kindness. Hoping Flora wouldn't act *too* kind, giving away the fact that she practically never had a friend to visit, Erin at the same time felt a rush of love. The tea tray looked so pretty. Cocoa in a blue pot, little sandwiches, some homemade cookies. She's trying to turn it into a sort of party, Erin realized, and hoped it wouldn't result in just seeming pathetic.

But Seti appeared not to find it anything of the kind. He ate and drank and looked at the fire with enthusiasm. He was so relaxed that it was impossible in his presence to worry that you'd say the wrong thing or make a fool of yourself without trying.

"I wonder," he said, "if Fred really means to make this movie. What do you think?"

"I think he gets a charge out of planning. But he doesn't stick to things too much. Just the same, it's a new camera and he'll want to do something with it. I don't think they'll let him use it in the museum."

"Why didn't you tell him?"

Erin looked at the floor. "I don't tell them—that gang—much of anything."

"Of course," he mused, "it would take old Fred a month to find a frog in his pocket."

Erin yelped with laughter. "Oh, Seti," she shrieked. "Oh, my goodness, that's so funny—"

Seti looked moderately pleased at this reaction to his sally. Also puzzled, Erin thought weakly, laughter abruptly cut off. She was doing just what she was always warning her about. Hooting.

Oh, it was all so difficult. How did people get from one day to the next? She began to wish he'd go. What was it Piglet had said, riding in Kanga's pocket as she bounded toward home? "If this is flying I shall never really take to it." Well, if this is friendship—

"Did you ever read Winnie-the-Pooh?" she barked.

"Oh, sure. When I was a kid."

"Well, I didn't mean now, for goodness' sakes. I just wondered if they had it in Egypt."

"Sure. We have lots of books."

"I didn't mean that—not the way it sounded. Honestly."

"What kind of books do you like to read?"

"History," Erin said promptly, deciding to leave out books like *Alice*, since it might seem to Seti another children's book, even though her father said it was for all ages, and she herself pretty much thought it was for none. "I've read lots of ancient Egyptian history."

"You have?" he said, sounding pleased. "How come?"

"My father is an Egyptologist *manqué*. That means he sells hormones for livestock, but what he really was meant to be was an archeologist, concentrating on the Nile Valley. He actually did go and work in some digs there years ago. Look, Seti," she said, getting up and walking to the glass case where her father kept his piece of ostraca. "Look at that."

"It's beautiful," he said. "It's authentic?"

"So far as Daddy knows. It was supposed to have been found outside a tomb in the Valley of the Nobles, just lying buried a little way down. Daddy says these things were like doodles to the artists."

"I'd like to meet your parents sometime."

"I'd love you to meet Daddy. You and he would have acres of stuff to say to each other."

"I guess my history lesson was old hat to you then."

"Pretty much," she admitted. "But it was interesting. I hadn't heard about the three-thousand-year trip from insect back to human being. That's interesting."

"If I'd lived somewhere toward the end of the Eighteenth Dynasty, that'd put me here just about now, wouldn't it?"

"Well, me, too. You said I looked Egyptian."

"What are your parents' ancestors?

"Daddy's people, sort of way back, were Scottish."

"And your mother?"

Erin lifted her shoulders. "American. Back to the Pilgrims, to hear her tell it. I don't think," she said, "that *that* sort of thing would have much to do with turning into a bug in ancient Egypt. I mean, you might end up *anywhere* after three thousand years."

"Those old Egyptians didn't plan to end up anywhere except right where they started. They considered anything else, anyplace else, abominable. Literally. They were always talking about the miserable Kush and the wretched Syrians and so forth. I don't think even an Egyptian bug would have left home."

"He might have been blown away on a wind and carried off to—well, to the Scottish Isles."

"He might, I guess," said Seti, laughing. "Well, I'd better go. Say, this has been awfully nice, Erin."

"I *loved* having you—I mean, I loved—well, yes—it's been awfully nice. I hope you—" She broke off, biting her lip. Stammering and blushing and behaving like an *ass*. Well, what could she ex*pect* of herself?

"What a nice boy," Flora said, when he'd gone.

"He's okay." Erin started upstairs, turned. "Flora, that was nice of you—to make such a nice cocoa party."

"It was my pleasure."

In her room Erin covered her face with her hands. She didn't know if she was happy or miserable. What sort of condition was that to be in, not even to know if she'd just had a good time or not?

CHAPTER TEN

"No," Flora was saying into the telephone. "Neither of them's here just now. No, I'm not sure when they'll be back. Shortly, I think. Yes, I'll leave a message saying you called."

"Why do you say you don't know when they'll be back?" Erin asked. "They'll be back Monday, you know that."

"Don't have to tell all you know to people. It's nobody's business where your parents are or when they'll be back. I tell the absolute basic minimum over the phone. In case it's burglars."

"Oh."

"That's one of their ways. They telephone to find out if people are home or if they're away how long they'll be gone, and then they just walk in and walk out with anything they want. Rich or poor, it's got so nobody's safe. Muggings, murders, robberies. What a world. Wasn't like this in my day."

Funny, Erin mused, how older people said "In my

day." As if with youth their day was gone, even when they were still alive and not old at all. When was a person's "day" over? Am I, she wondered, having my "day" *now*? What a discouraging thought.

"Were things really much better then, Flora?"

"They were. In a lot of ways, that is. I grew up in this city, and I used to ride the subways and busses all over town, and I was *never* scared. Didn't occur to me I had a reason to be. Now here I am a grown woman and I wouldn't go out after dark for any price. Hardly even like going out in the daytime."

"That's too bad. I was hoping we could go over to the museum and have lunch there. I love that cafeteria."

"Oh, we can do that, honey. It was just a figure of speech, sort of, and besides, the museum's only a few blocks away. But in the old days I'd have taken you— oh, maybe down to the Battery on the subway and then across to Staten Island on the ferry. I remember when those ferries were clean. And a fellow walked around playing an accordion. Lovely, it was."

"Couldn't we do that, Flora? It might still be fun."

"Might be the end of us, too. No, we're taking no subways, just the two of us. Or ferries."

"Okay." Erin sighed, then brightened. She did love the Metropolitan and the cafeteria with the big shallow pond in the center with skinny greeny statues for fountains. If you were lucky, you could get a table right next to the pool. *"Au bord du lac,"* her father always said when he took her there and they snared a poolside place. The first time that had struck her as so funny that she'd choked on her Coke, laughing. Her father didn't seem to mind her laugh—no light and airy chime, but something that made lots of people wince.

("Can't you *try* to control that—that *braying*, Erin? Can't you hear how it *sounds*?")

Erin could hear and did try to control it. Sometimes she decided never to laugh again in her whole life. A little smile, at most. That was what she'd permit herself. A secret little tantalizing smile. But *no* laughter. She'd written this down in her notebook, where she kept admonitions to herself. "Remember not to laugh," she'd written. "Even if something's very funny." And she'd added, with inflexible self-criticism, "Or even if you're very nervous."

Much good it did. The laugh was a mechanism inside her. Self-start and self-destruct. She didn't have her finger on the button, so how could she control it? I wish I were grown-up, she thought, trudging upstairs to change from blue jeans into a dress, because Flora wouldn't take her anyplace on her jeans. The whole museum was going to be full of kids in sloppy clothes, but she was lucky to get away with not wearing gloves. And *she,* much younger than Flora, was just as bad. Don't they ever look and *see* how things are? Erin wondered. Don't they know that I'm the only girl in New York City who's forced to wear a dress every time she steps out the door?

It would be better to be grown-up, even if it meant that your "day" would be over. When I'm grown, I'm going to dress the way I want, and laugh the way I want, and to hell with anyone who doesn't like it. I'm going to live alone, anyway. Except for a cat, or maybe two cats. Possibly fifty. I'll have a house in the country in the middle of a hundred acres and I'll run around naked *and* laughing if I want to.

She never could decide whether she wanted to grow up or not. In some ways it seemed a good idea. You'd be free of people, on your own. But in other ways—wouldn't it be pretty scary? Being on her own and free of people? At least now she had her father and Flora. Who would she have then?

Oh, it all seemed, sometimes, too difficult. Figuring things out, trying to make something of yourself. Trying, as *she* would put it, "To *cope*." "I simply cannot *cope*," *she*'d say, putting her fingers to her temples. *She* got migraines. Such a classy ailment. Erin put her fingers to her forehead, hoping for a twinge. She couldn't ask for a migraine, of course, but even an ordinary headache would suffice. Something that would allow her to crawl into bed and shut out the world. But her head wouldn't ache, and Flora was waiting.

At first, fortune smiled on them. They got a table all to themselves, *au bord du lac*. They watched the water running down the length of the marvelous emaciated fauns in the pond and planned where in the museum they'd go when they felt they'd kept the table long enough.

They went first to look at furniture in the American Wing, Flora's favorite. Then to the Egyptian rooms, with Flora grumbling about having to look at coffins. "Seems all those ancient Egyptians ever gave any thought to was dying."

"Flora, that isn't so. Don't you ever listen to Daddy?"

"I listen. And then I come over here and look at coffins. Coffins speak louder than words."

Erin giggled. "No, but just the same. Look at all

this beautiful jewelry, and the golden goblets. And that silver mirror with the bronze handle. And that gorgeous bronze cat with the earrings. What about that cat?"

"That gorgeous bronze cat," Flora said, "is a mummy case. I read it on the description."

"Oh, well. If you're going to be like that."

"I'm sorry," Flora said, relenting. "And you and your father are right. This is beautiful stuff. Even the coffins are, with all those marvelous little pictures on them. And the colors!"

"I wish I could read hieroglyphics. Wouldn't that be fun, to be able to read and write in hieroglyphics?"

Walking through the several vast rooms that housed the Metropolitan's Egyptian collection, Erin stopped now and then for a moment, trying to think herself back to the time when a hand now dust for thousands of years had actually held a brush, painting the long eyes of Aau Neferu, here before her. She tried to feel in her own fingers the sensation of the artist who had drawn and colored the little crouching hare and the flying bird on the panel from Aau Neferu's tomb. They had been brought all these centuries later to this place in this land the Egyptians could not have dreamed of and would have detested, to be put under glass and stared at by her, Erin Gandy.

"I wish," she had said to her father, walking here with him one day, "that everything, just about, wasn't under glass. That bronze cat with the gold earrings. Wouldn't it be nice to be able to touch her, to touch something that old and beautiful?"

"When I was a boy the things here weren't so glassed in. The cat was, I believe. But the wall panels in the mastaba, those were touchable then. Probably that's why they're under glass now. Too many of us wanting to touch the past. And then, the usual vandals who scratch their initials on any accessible surface started doing their moronic thing here."

"Weren't there vandals when you were a boy?"

"There have always been vandals, by whatever name they were called. Napoleon's soldiers carved their initials on the Sphinx and used its great face for target practice. Wouldn't surprise me if Herodotus scratched his initials on some colossus somewhere."

Now Erin regarded Aau Neferu and tried to see Seti in him someplace. There was one point of resemblance. An air of calm. Seti seemed so in touch with himself—not spacy and full of sprung springs jangling every which way. It seemed to her, looking at him, that Aau Neferu might well have been the same type.

"Flora, before we leave, could we go in the postcard room and the bookshop?"

"Of course."

Erin found a postcard of the bronze cat with gold earrings. In the bookshop she found a paperback that undertook to teach anyone to write hieroglyphics.

"See, I *could* learn. I think I'll buy this—"

At that moment some all-too-familiar voices came to her from the other side of the rack that was too high to see over. She didn't need to see Fred, Faith, Rosemary, Ed, and Seti to know them. She could only pray they wouldn't come around and find her with Flora, who looked, all at once, like a governess. The rest of them were out on their own, doing things together, but she was spending her Saturday afternoon being taken to the museum like a child. Even as she thought it she felt a sense of disloyalty. Only moments before she and Flora had been two friends out together for the afternoon, and now—

But she had to get out of here. "Flora, let's—"

She stopped, hearing Fred's voice lifted above the others. His voice was changing, and it often wavered toward shrillness when he was annoyed or excited. He appeared to be both now.

"That grotty bunch in the stupid office—I asked them, polite as pie, if we could make part of our movie here, I mean with hand-*held* cameras, which people are allowed to have for *stills*, and they said not a chance."

"But why?" said Rosemary. "We're doing something original and creative. I thought that was supposed to be encouraged in us."

"Well, think again. The dumbfool woman said we couldn't *act* for the cameras, and we couldn't wear *costumes*, but we could stand in front of the cameras in our regular clothes if it was a time when there weren't too many people around and if—oh, bull."

"Did you tell her you can't make a movie about ancient Egypt if you can only stand still in your blue jeans?"

"Yeah," said Ed. "I mean, I think we'd lose a certain element of authenticity—"

"I told her, all right. She said if they allowed *us* to wear costumes and act, then they'd have to allow fashion models in and other types wanting to use museum backgrounds to sell their glue."

"Glue?"

"Oh, whatever they're selling."

"Didn't you tell her we aren't selling anything?"

"Sure I told her. I told her all kinds of things, and it adds up to no soap."

"That's a darned *shame*," Rosemary said.

"Ah—who cares about their grubby museum. They've got practically everything under glass anyway so there'd probably be too many reflections. Anyway—I've got another idea. We'll scrap ancient Egypt and do a movie out in the park."

"About what?"

"We'll think of something. A murder story. How about that?"

"You'll have to have a role for Erin Gandy," Seti said. "You primised her."

At the sound of her name, Erin's face reddened. She glanced at Flora, hoping she hadn't heard. She had. Erin wanted to run but felt as if her shoes had been nailed to the floor.

"Say, what gives with you and that little creep?" Fred asked. "You got a case on her or something?"

"Oh, Fred!" said Faith and Rosemary, their voices merry. "A case on Blowfish Gandy! Whatever will you think of next?"

"Now, cut it out," Seti said. "She's a nice girl—"

"She's a pushy little clot, always wanting to get *in* with people."

"Doesn't everybody want to get in with people?" Seti asked sharply.

"Seti, I can't make you out. You sound like a be-kind-to-dumb-animals crusader."

"Don't call another human being an animal!"

"She laughs like a hyena, doesn't she? And makes faces like a fish? So doesn't that make her—"

"You," said Seti, "make me sick. If you'll excuse me I don't want to be part of your movie."

Shoving aside Flora's arm, which had gone around her shoulders in a gesture of reassurance, Erin ran from the room, from Flora, from her *schoolmates*, from awareness, from the world. *Somehow she would get away, away, away—*

She ran blindly toward the mastaba, pitched into it headlong, and butted her forehead on a limestone corner. Reeling, she plunged into the entrance, turned to the left, and found herself in a cul-de-sac from which there was no escape.

"Oh, God," she sobbed. "Daddy! Somebody! Save me!"

A voice—Flora's? Seti's?—called to her from a distance.

"Erin! Erin!"

They were coming after her. Flora and Seti. All of them, maybe. To laugh, or to say they hadn't really meant it, or—

"Bastet! Cat Queen! Save me!"

She put her hands against the glassed wall panel, seeing her wild reflection there, as though in a mirror. She pressed against it, sobbing.

PART TWO

CHAPTER ELEVEN

"Irun! Irun!"

Ignoring the voice, Irun put her hands to her head, which pained most dreadfully. At last she'd got a headache. At last? What did she mean by that? Who wanted to get a headache? And what was all this—this mass of hair around her? She felt the kinky substance carefully. Had she put on someone's wig? She pulled hard and winced. It was her own, but how had it got there? How had it got so long and tangly?

Where was she, and why? What had *happened*? She'd been running. Running from something that troubled her, hurt her. She remembered that much.

Now she lay on the burning sand, and Fl'ret's voice was urging her, calling her. "Irun, Irun—open your eyes!"

Cautiously she lifted her lids a slit, peered into Fl'ret's anxious face, then glanced around. She was in front of the ancient mastaba of Ha'tpet, Keeper of the

King's Vineyards, who'd lived long ago in the time when nobles still built these mastabas near their homes.

This Ha'tpet had been an ancestor of her own father, Perub, Keeper of the King's Vineyards himself, and the family still brought offerings of food here to his tomb on feast days.

Today was not a feast day. And the mastaba was well away from the great house where Perub and his family and servants lived. It stood, this tomb, almost on the edge of the eastern desert. The house of Ha'tpet, to which it had been attached, had long returned to dust, as an earthly house should, leaving the resting place of limestone and granite to stand through eternity.

But what am *I* doing here? Irun asked herself again. I have nothing to do with Ha'tpet on a day that is not a feast day, so why am I lying on the hot sand next to his old mastaba?

"Why am I here?" she mumbled. "What am I doing here? And what is all this on my head?"

"Open your eyes," Fl'ret said again, and when at length Irun forced her lids up, the woman's eyes peered intently into hers. Beyond her stood Seti, handsome brow furrowed. His smooth-shaven head gleamed in the sun. Fl'ret's wig was askew.

"Everything's askew," said Irun faintly.

Fl'ret motioned to a servant standing nearby.

"Take her up gently, Ayu, and carry her to the master's house. No jogging, mind. Irun, do not go to sleep again. Who knows how long you have been lying here in the desert? It is good that the shade of your ancestor's tomb protected you from the rays of the Sun God. That," she said with satisfaction, "is what comes of scrupulously remembering one's ancestors at the proper times."

"What do you mean, who knows how long?" Irun asked irritably. She felt comfortable and safe in Ayu's strong arms and happy to be going home, but she could not understand what had happened, and not understanding made her cross.

Fl'ret replied in a tart voice. "I am your servant, my little ibis. Not your shadow. I can't know what you are doing every moment of the day. Seti says he has been looking for you for hours, since you ran away from the Temple School, where you were hanging around the entrance again, telling people that girls, too, should be allowed to go to school and learn to read and write. Isis! Where do you *get* these notions?"

Irun didn't answer. She knew she was notional, and knew no more than Fl'ret did where the notions came from. Yet she burned with the desire to read and write. She glanced at Seti, trotting along beside Ayu. He was looking at her anxiously.

Now she remembered. She'd been walking in the outer courtyard of the Great Temple—where anyone, even women and girls, even commoners and slaves, was permitted to walk. She'd been gazing across the lake to the sacred orchard of persea and acacia trees, palms and flowering fruit trees, thinking how beautiful it was over there and how awesome here in the vast colonnaded courtyard. She'd had no special destination in mind, no plans. When her father was away, as he was now, she always felt aimless.

Then what had happened? Fuzzily she recalled that Fayet and Semary, two of the five daughters of Piankhy, the Vizier, had come running by with Seti, son of the Governor of the nome, and Edzme, son of the

Royal Chamberlain, and a couple of other boys. The boys had been on their way to the Temple School, where they were studying under the Royal Scribe. Had she tried to go into the school with them? Yes, she rather thought she had. She'd done it before. She recalled yelling at them that she was just as entitled to learn as they were, and at that they'd begun to laugh—except Seti—and those two pretty and idiotic girls had simpered and minced around, giggling.

"She thinks because she has a head like an ibis, she should imitate Thoth and become a scribe!"

"A woman scribe! Oh, oh, it is too funny!"

The boys, hearing their fraction-witted comments, had begun to slap their thighs with amusement, until Seti rebuked them. "Only a fool wounds another's feelings and laughs at another's hopes. Someone will laugh at *his* feelings and hopes one day, too."

This speech seemed to redouble their amusement. "Oh, Seti! Wise One! You would defend all, even the meanest, even a sparrow! A girl scribe! Oh, oh, oh—"

Their raucous laughter had echoed in the Temple courtyard. It rang like a series of blows in Irun's head. It must have been then, she thought, remembering the scene mistily, uncertainly, that I ran. And ran and ran. Away from the temple and those tormentors, along the Nile bank where the shouts of sailors and chants of rowers made the river ring, through the teeming marketplace, and so out to the very edge of the desert where the ancient, isolated mastaba of Ha'tpet confronted the eternal sands.

Ayu carried her gently, but her headache seemed to increase with each step he took. She moaned and heard Fl'ret say to Seti, "Run to your father's mansion and get the doctor. Ask him to come immediately to the house of Perub. Go now, quickly."

"I'll bring him," Seti called over his shoulder, already on his way.

"Don't bring him, just send him," Fl'ret cried out, and shook her head. "He's a streak. He moves like a lizard. How are you feeling, little lotus?"

"Not like a flower," Irun said weakly. Like a dying rat, she thought, and added aloud, "How would I know what a rat felt like when it was dying? Or when it was not dying?"

"Wandering," Fl'ret said with alarm. "I hope that doctor is prompt. Be careful, Ayu! Take care!"

They were at the mansion now. They went through the great gate of the outer wall, across the outer yard, into the cool columned hall, along the gallery surrounding the inner courtyard, past the pool where carp swam and fountains rustled, and so to the women's quarters, where Ayu laid Irun gently on her own bed and retired without a sound.

Fl'ret brought a basin of scented water and bathed Irun's flushed face and body. Handling the mass of dusty, sweat-drenched hair, she said, "This is no mystery, this. You've been bewitched. How else could your hair have grown down past your shoulders in a matter of hours? Bedeviled. What will your father say?"

"I want it *off*, Fl'ret! Fetch a razor and cut it *off*!" After that first tug, Irun had kept her hands away from the frightening mass of hair, but the weight of it was making her head pound.

Fl'ret put a plump hand on Irun's forehead. "We must wait for the doctor. He must see this evidence of bewitchment. You have a fever. There is sweat on your brow and it is hot, very hot. I *wish* that doctor would come."

"Where's my father, Fl'ret?" Irun moaned.

"Yes, it is clear you are sick and wandering in your wits. You know your father went to the Greater Oasis many days ago to see to the grape harvest there."

"Did *she* go with him?"

"By she, you mean your lady mother?"

"You know who I mean. She. Her. My father's wife."

"Your mother."

"All *right*. Did she?"

"Of course. And you know that, as well. You are asking these questions to which you know the answers either because your mind is disordered, or because you wish simply to upset me . . . I, who am already distracted." The woman ran her hand down Irun's arms and legs. "Sweating all over." She rose. "Lie there. I shall send El-oy in to sit with you until I return with the doctor."

"I don't need anyone to sit with me."

But Fl'ret was gone, and in a moment young El-oy glided in and sat on the cool tile floor, leaning against the wall. She did not speak or even, after one quick glance, look at Irun. Like Ayu, she was a slave and did not speak unless addressed. Irun, confused and terrified to a degree she had not confided to Flora—*Flora?* Who was *Flora?*—to Fl'ret, Fl'ret, *Fl'ret*—did not think to speak to El-oy. She must know the girl, and yet she did not know her.

She knew this house, and yet it seemed strange. Knew herself—yet she seemed to be inhabiting the body of a stranger. Fl'ret must be right. Her wits were wandering. My wits have wandered so far they are altogether gone. Maybe, she thought with a shiver, her ka-t had got out of her body and taken wing and now had come back tired and confused, not knowing how to get back inside. She stared miserably around the room, half expecting to see her ka-t fluttering like a stricken bird. But if it was there—her ka-t spirit—it was invisible and made no sound.

The thing to do was lie very still and not think. Just lie and listen to the fountains singing in the courtyard, to the hoopoe bird singing in the acacia tree. Lie still, and wait for the doctor to come and summon her being back to her body. She watched little lizards darting up the walls, across the ceiling. Some red as carnelian, some bluey-grey, others green as feldspar. They sparked across her vision, outlines blurred by the tears that rolled down her temples into the awful hair. Possessed by a demon. How frightening it was, and how terrible, terrible. Maybe even the doctor would not, with his best medicine and magic, be able to make her whole again. And if he could not, what would happen to her?

What had happened to her?

She must have fallen senseless out there in the desert. And she was senseless still, if to have sense is to know who you are, and where you are, and why. I seem to be myself, she thought, yet not to be myself, and Fl'ret is the only one I know, and yet she, too, seems not to be herself.

She felt the bed swing slowly beneath her, as if she were on a little boat on the river, swaying in the waves—

She closed her eyes.

From somewhere far off she heard a voice calling. *"Erin, Erin, can you hear me? I'm here with you."*

"Irun, Irun, can you hear me?"

She opened her eyes lazily, unwillingly, and met the fixed dark eyes of Pepi, the Governor's physician. He loomed over her, looking grave and keen. He carried a bag, which he set on the floor a little distance from Irun's bed.

Before he could speak or begin his examination, Irun said, "Fl'ret, do you feel yourself to be yourself? *Tell me, please.*"

"That's a strange question, child," said Fl'ret, looking at the doctor, who nodded. "Strange, indeed."

"What do you mean by that?" he asked attentively.

Irun sighed. "Nobody seems real. No, Fl'ret—not you, not El-oy there. Not you, doctor. And I—I think I don't belong here, but I don't know where I do belong—someplace else, sometime else," she said, her lids falling again, voice growing drowsy. "Everything seems to be going around," she murmured. "Nothing stays *still.*"

The doctor put his strong hand on her brow, then over her heart. "This is an ailment I will treat," he said to Fl'ret, who gave a nervous sob of relief. Sometimes, after feeling the head and the heart of an afflicted person, a doctor said, "This is an ailment I cannot treat."

"Doctor," said Fl'ret, "you may not have seen Irun very often—"

"I have seen her," said the doctor, stooping to open his bag.

"Then you must know that she has, like other girl children, normal hair. Short to the scalp, with a side lock. Not this mess that looks like the Governor's wig. Meaning no disrespect, of course," she added quickly.

"On the Governor, such a wig is an adornment, but on a child—"

"I take your meaning," said the doctor. He looked at El-oy. "Fetch a razor, girl."

El-oy went to an inlaid cabinet that stood against the wall and brought forth a bronze razor, ivory-handled. Like the bronze-handled silver mirror that matched it, this razor was very old. It had belonged to Irun's mother, Bel, wife of Perub, and to her mother before her, and to her mother before that. Nonetheless, the razor was marvelously sharp, and when, with a comb in one hand and the razor in the other, the doctor in swift strokes attacked Irun's wiry mass of hair, it fell away quickly in a tangled heap on the tile floor. The doctor directed Fl'ret to gather up even the tiniest strand and then to burn the whole to ashes, which she was then to seal in a tiny urn, burying that in the garden.

"This unusual growth of hair," he explained, "has been caused by the demon within. Once the hair is burned, sealed, and buried, she will not be able to sow such another crop."

Fl'ret directed El-oy to gather up the hair and place it in a bowl and then it was put to one side. Fl'ret, Irun supposed, would not trust El-oy to attend to the burning and burial as closely as she should.

For her part, Irun already felt better, with that heaviness gone from her head. She felt light-headed, giddy with relief, and made a move to leave her bed so as to look in the silver mirror. As she sat up, the room swung in a great arc. Had Fl'ret not caught her, she would have pitched forward to the floor.

"Lie back," the doctor directed. "Do not attempt to rise until I give you leave."

"All right," Irun said faintly. She put her head back on the carved wooden neck rest, ran her hands over the short shorn hair. It felt so good. She sighed, watching the doctor idly, wondering whether his medicine would drive the dizziness from her head as easily as he'd removed the hair from it.

He spread out on the tile floor a string of blue faïence beads, a clay amulet in the shape of a girl child, a mortar and pestle, some jars of oil and unguent, a few sprigs of herbs. Not looking at her, he passed his hands over the amulet, ran the beads through his fingers, saying softly an incantation known to his profession.

Then he sat back on his heels, fixed his gaze on Irun's and intoned: **"O Re, O Aten, O Shu, O Geb, O Nut, O Anubis who is before the Devine Shrine, O Horus, O Set, O Isis, O Nephthys, O Great Ennead, O Little Ennead, come ye to remove that enemy, dead man or dead woman, male adversary or female adversary, who is in the face of Irun, born of woman, Bel!"**

He placed a piece of fine linen upon Irun's face and continued.

"O this demon that is within this child, quit her on the moment! I, Pepi, the Governor's Physician, command you!"

He placed the amulet over Irun's heart and draped the beads across her brow.

"In the name of Re, Aten, Shu, Geb, Nut, Anubis, Horus, Set, Isis, Nephthys, the Great Ennead, the Little Ennead, GO!"

Fl'ret stood with her hands twisting together. El-oy stood with her eyes cast down. The doctor crouched with his gaze on Irun while the sun, falling through a high window, advanced a fraction of an inch up the wall, which was painted with a scene of wildfowling in the marshes. The bar of sun reached toward the tip of a goose's wing, then touched it with light, before the doctor stirred.

"Stronger measures are called for. I shall apply the next remedy." He removed the beads and the linen cloth from Irun's face, the amulet from her chest. He got a little wicker cage of beetles from his bag. Deftly extracting one big ebony shining insect, he cast it into his mortar, and before the thing could wriggle away, mashed it with his pestle. "A measure of the oil of the castor bean," he muttered, "plus the beetle, finely ground, plus—" He put a finger to his cheek and considered.

Irun, watching these preparations uneasily, wondered what he planned to do with the concoction. Rub it on her? *That'll be the end of the string,*" she mumbled. "*Massaged with a mashed beetle. Cripes.*"

Fl'ret clasped her hands above her head and looked at the doctor in terror. "Possessed! She is wholly and utterly possessed! O Great Isis! My poor little girl! What will her father say? She's babbling words unknown to man."

"Woman, be quiet! Child, open your mouth!"

Irun gulped and gagged. Oh, *no* . . . no, no, no, no, *no!*

"I'm better now!" she screamed. "I do not, revered sir, the Governor's physician, require the ground beetle and the oil of the castor bean and the—"

The doctor nodded patiently at the girl's impertinence, a symptom which demonstrated how firmly the demon was entrenched. The girl herself would not dare question a doctor's procedure.

"When the hostile spirit that is lodged in your body

tastes this preparation, then she'll be glad enough to quit, I can assure you. I shall add two pits from the bitter apple tree. No," he repeated confidently, "your demon will not find this prescription to her taste."

"I'm not going to find it to mine either," Irun wailed. "I have to taste it before the demon does!"

Fl'ret's hand moved nervously as if to halt the flow of Irun's words, but the doctor shook his head. "It is not the child who speaks," he said kindly. "It is the demon within. Still—" He touched his finger delicately to the mixture in the mortar, touched the finger to his tongue, wiped his tongue with the back of his hand. "Since she is a child, I shall add something to make it taste good. In any case, better. Anise, I think." He opened one of his little alabaster jars and the odor of licorice floated into the room as he added a touch of anise to his nostrum. He did not, Irun observed, taste it again.

"If, of course, this does not have the desired effect," he said to Fl'ret, "I shall be obliged to resort to stricter measures yet."

Stricter than beetles? Irun thought weakly. The doctor was talking as if she couldn't hear. She had the impression that he considered that she, a child, like El-oy, a slave, could not comprehend the words of a being so exalted as himself. But she could hear him, all right.

"A chopped mouse," he was saying. "Or even"—he spoke with enthusiasm—"a live mouse. Getting this one to swallow a live mouse might prove difficult—"

"Difficult?" said Fl'ret in a carrying whisper. "It will be impossible. Quite impossible."

"Nothing," said the doctor, "is impossible to medicine."

Irun closed her eyes. "Bastet!" she pleaded silently. "Cat Goddess! Deliver me from the mouse, I implore you!"

With a horn spoon, Pepi, the physician, offered the beetle mixture to Irun, who looked wildly at Fl'ret, finding no help in that stern face—a sternness that was partly fear for Irun, partly awe of the doctor, and partly dismay that she had been obliged to handle this problem on her own in the absence of Perub and his wife. Irun knew this, but still she burst out, "Please, Fl'ret—oh, *please*. I cannot swallow—"

The doctor took advantage of her open mouth to thrust the horn spoon in and then, withdrawing it quickly, clapped his hand over her face so that she was forced to swallow.

Oh, vile . . . *hideously vile—*

She began to gag, and Fl'ret, with an imperious gesture, summoned El-oy, who had already picked up a bowl in readiness. Irun leaned over and lost the mess, then lay back panting while Fl'ret wiped her face with perfumed water.

The doctor looked pleased and gratified. He gathered up his jars and implements, his wicker cage of beetles, his mortar and pestle, and put them carefully back in his bag. His own servants would attend to the rearrangement of these, under his supervision.

Getting to his feet, he said in a deep voice, passing his hands above Irun's limp form, "One can observe that the hostile spirit was spewed forth as a result of my medication. A cure has been effected, praise be to Imhotep.

"I shall leave the amulet and the beads," he said in a more normal voice to Fl'ret. "See that the child rests here until morning, taking no food, but only a little watered wine to remove the taste of the demon."

To remove the taste of your medicine, Irun thought morosely. She closed her eyes, miserably conscious that the doctor's medicine had not driven forth the demon, because she was still thinking the same lost thoughts. *What is this place and what am I doing here?* she wondered one moment, and then, the next, Why, it is the mansion of my father, Perub, and I am here because I am his daughter and belong here.

I don't belong here!

But where, then where?

The sunlight by now had left the wall and lay in the gradually receding bar across the ceiling. Fl'ret had gone off with the bowl of horrible hair, saying she'd be back, and silent El-oy was no more company, or disturbance, than one of the painted figures in the mural or one of the jewel-like lizards that ran across it.

Irun got shakily from her bed and began to totter about the room, trying to make it hers, make herself belong in it. She looked for a long time at the wall painting, at the birds flying—one of them falling to a throw stick—at the hunters, men, women, and children crowded in the skiff. They were accompanied by a cat who was in the marshes, about to retrieve the falling bird. There were herons and hoopoes and geese crowding the air, and stands of papyrus growing thickly, lotus flowers floating on the water, beneath which fish went swarming past. A scene that was familiar to her. She'd been to the marshes with her father. And with *her. She* went wherever Perub went, just about.

"My lady mother," Irun muttered, and then, "*Her.*"

114

That sounded better. They said of her that she resembled Nefertiti, that beautiful queen of the peculiar Pharaoh Akhnaten, who had turned his back on his ancestors and his ancestors' gods and moved the court away from Thebes to a place far down the Nile, where he built the town of Akhetaten and lived in isolation from the people and indifferent to them. He had been so hated that when he died the people and the priests destroyed his town, Akhetaten, entirely, and moved the capital back to Thebes. But Nefertiti's beauty seemed to excuse her all. She was remembered proudly and spoken of with reverence. Beauty, thought Irun. Beauty matters. Maybe it is all that matters.

She turned her gaze from the wall to the room. The furniture was at once simple and lovely. Her bed a narrow frame of dark wood painted brightly and strung with bands of white linen. Two stools of the same wood and linen, legs carved to represent those of herons. The chest, polished and intricate with inlay. The floor was tiled in blue and cool to her bare feet. Along the wall facing the colonnaded courtyard was a bead curtain. Irun staggered to it and separated the strands. Out of the corner of her eye she caught a gesture from El-oy.

"I'm not leaving," she said. "Just looking."

She stood, swaying, looking out. The courtyard was vast, with rows of lotus columns supporting the ambulatory and the loggia above it—a flat porch that she could not see but remembered. In the great central court the pool reflected the blue plain of heaven. Fountains plumed at either end. There were carp swimming in there, dark golden fish of great size, and blue lotus blossoms opened their cups to the sun. Beyond all this, in the outer walled courtyard that separated this dwelling from the streets, there were, Irun knew, acacias and dom palms and perseas and pomegranate trees. She could see tall palm fronds, motionless as sculptured columns. Everything out there was still, very still. Except for a hoopoe bird singing and the fountain waters falling there was no sound, no motion.

She looked up at the sky where the sun, too white to gaze at, seemed directly overhead. She turned back into the room. El-oy, sitting with her back to the wall, was asleep. No doubt everyone in this house of her father was resting or asleep now, except for herself and Fl'ret. Perhaps she, too, should lie down again and try to rest or to sleep.

But drawn, as she'd known she would be, to the silver mirror, she stepped noiselessly up to it, stood with her head averted for a moment, then picked it up and looked to see what face, what person, she must encounter there.

A girl. Well, yes. That, at least, did not surprise her. She was a girl. What girl? Herself. Who was that, this *herself*? She peered into the mirror's silver face, searching for her own. A girl with short dark hair, a thin face with a prominent but not unpleasing nose, dark long eyes. This girl looked out from the mirror with a challenging expression and Irun challenged her back. *They* knew, the two of them, that the demon was still within, trying to confuse them. Succeeding. Irun, daughter of Perub, Keeper of the King's Vineyards. Or—somebody else entirely. Or somebody else, partly.

"I don't know you," Irun said softly. "But maybe you know me?"

116

How many mirrors had she looked in, walked through? *Walked through?* What a notion. If she said anything like that to Flora—to *Fl'ret*, that was—why the Governor's physician would be summoned back and this time might make her swallow a chopped-up mouse. Or a live mouse, she thought hysterically. It would run around inside her. It would—

She went dizzily to the bed and lay down again. What she would do was—nothing. Say not a word of her wild thoughts to anyone. What she feared was that somehow, by a dreadful mischance, her ka-t had taken leave of her body and was now wandering through space, through time, trying surely to get back to her. Surely *trying!* Irun did not think that the doctor or his medicine or his magic would lure her ka-t back to its home. She would have to be patient and silent and wait, be ready at any time with a welcome for her unfortunate spirit. Then this unsteadiness of head and uncertainty of mind would pass. Would surely pass.

Meanwhile, she would be obliged to live with her demon.

Meanwhile, too, she liked the look of her hair. "*Kind of an Afro,*" she said to herself, almost aloud. "*Really mod.*" She did not ask herself where she had got such mad unknown words as *Afro* and *mod*.

She didn't ask herself anything further. She fell asleep.

CHAPTER TWELVE

Perub and his wife returned that evening from the oasis where he had been inspecting the wine grapes of the King. A runner preceded them by several hours in order that any slackness of attention on the part of the household might be pulled taut before the arrival of the master. The corridors and kitchens began a hive-like humming and industry as a fine meal was readied. Throughout the many halls and rooms, the large courtyard and the smaller one, the stables and orchard, members of the household busied themselves at tasks that had not, in fact, been much neglected in the absence of Perub. Unlike some nobles, Perub did not have the practice of trying to surprise his people in unauthorized relaxation, thereby giving himself an opportunity to rage and rebuke and punish. Perub never raged, rarely rebuked, and even more rarely punished.

Fl'ret was helping Irun to dress, in case she should

be summoned to her mother's presence, although there was no certainty that she would be.

"Your lady mother," Fl'ret said, making excuses in advance, "may well be too tired to receive, directly after her journey's end."

I don't care, Irun thought. Just so I see my father.

She was wearing a freshly starched short white skirt of fine linen. She was bare from the waist up and thought her little breasts looked like bubbles. Vaguely she wished that she could cover them, then wondered why she'd wished it. Even when they did cover their breasts, Egyptian women wore linen of so delicate a texture that they might as well have been uncovered.

I am really so confused, she thought. So tangled and disordered. The thing was—to keep this from them. She bit her lip, wondering if she could confide in Fl'ret. Tell her that the demon had not gone forth with the beetle brew. But she dared not. Fl'ret would consider it her duty to report to Perub, and the Governor's physician would be called back, more remedies applied—horrible to contemplate—and if *those* proved also vain, then what would she do? What would they do to or about her?

"That *man*," Fl'ret grumbled. "I should not have let him cut your hair, doctor or no doctor. I should have done it myself. He has neglected to leave you a side lock to hang over your ear. Wait now—" She rummaged in the chest. "There must be one here somewhere. Ah, here it is." She held aloft a twist of hair. "A curl left over from one of your mother's wigs. I'll just fasten it with this lovely pin. And now a little collar, and you are quite ready. There, look at yourself."

Irun looked in the mirror. Her lips curved in a slow

smile. The collar of colored beads was narrow, not one of the impressive broad collars of gold and semi-precious stones worn by women, but it was pretty, and the butterfly pin holding the curl that hung over her left ear was pretty.

"Don't I look nice," she said, and Fl'ret clapped her hands with pleasure.

"You must be healed of the accident. I withdraw any slur I cast upon Pepi. He is a very Imhotep. You look in the mirror and know yourself and know your self to be comely. And that is a cure, certainly, if ever a cure made itself manifest."

She's trying hard to convince one of us, Irun thought, but was willing to be convinced.

"Still," Fl'ret added with a sigh, "I shall have to inform your father."

"But, Fl'ret—"

"It is of no use to argue with me, child. Even if I were inclined to keep the matter silent, and I might be so inclined, seeing how *well* you are," she insisted, "the Governor's physician will send his bill, and then I should have to explain why it was necessary to call him here in your father's absence. It is wiser to explain at once a matter that will require explanation in any case."

"Very wise," Irun said glumly.

"I should think your father and mother would be arriving in their chariot at any moment. Why don't you run to the great gate to greet them?"

Irun looked around wildly. All day she had remained in this room, except to go a couple of times to the earth closet, which was down an attached passageway, and of course to spend some time in the room adjoining, where she'd stepped down into the stone tub and sloshed about happily while Fl'ret poured perfumed water over her.

She'd remained in here because it was the only place she felt sure of. If she left this room, went out and began to wander around that vast layout of rooms and courts and corridors and gardens, she might get lost. She didn't know whether she knew this estate well enough to find her way back to this room once she'd lost sight of it. Just as bad was the sense of having the floor sway beneath her feet, of having her head reel a little all the time. Whether she stood or lay down, the feeling persisted. Suppose she went out there and fell down again, as she'd fallen down near the mastaba?

Oh, I don't know what to do—and I am frightened, frightened.

"Come, now," said Fl'ret, taking her arm. "Let us go to the gate." She turned abruptly and looked into Irun's eyes. "Child, you have been deceiving me. You are not well yet. I felt you sway under my touch like a reed in the breeze."

That's how I feel, Irun thought. A reed in the breeze. No will but the breeze's will. "I'm *better*, Fl'ret."

"I think you are not speaking the truth."

Irun grabbed the woman's arm. "Fl'ret, please. Maybe I am a little dizzy still, but each moment I am surer of who I am—I mean, I am steadier than the moment before. Please, do not tell them."

"I have explained. I must."

"I mean, do not tell them that the doctor's medicine didn't work. That it didn't work right *away*. Maybe it takes a while to work altogether, and pretty soon I shall be altogether myself." Myself, she thought. *My-*

self? But she had no time now to wonder about that. She must convince Fl'ret that the medicine would be effective, or the doctor would come again. Another visit from him and she wouldn't care if she were alive or dead.

"Fl'ret, Fl'ret, do you promise?" she asked, walking at the woman's side, not noticing where they were going. "Do you?"

"Yes, yes, all right," said Fl'ret at length. "I shall say that the doctor was here, and why. I shall describe his treatment and your reaction. Then—since you wish it—I shall let them decide for themselves if the physic was potent or no."

"Oh, thank you," Irun breathed. "Thank you, dear Fl'ret." She squeezed the servant's hand and had her own squeezed in return. With Fl'ret she was safe. With Fl'ret, she thought, I am loved.

"You wouldn't ever leave me, would you?" she asked.

"What a question. Why should I leave you?"

"Oh, things happen," Irun said vaguely. "Strange things. I mean, suppose I should die of this ailment. Or die of the treatment. Then I should have to go West without you, Fl'ret—all alone, all alone, all alone—"

"Nonsense. Your father would have my image made into a shabti that would go into your coffin with you. And I should serve you in that image until in due time I myself go West and join you. Something tells me I shall be with you through eternity."

"Isn't that *lovely*. Or—" with a quick glance at Fl'ret's face "—do you mind?"

"Why should I mind? There are those—I'll name no names—who chaff at the condition of serving others.

122

But when you think matters through to the logical endpoint, you find that everyone is a servant. Your father, the Governor, the Vizier himself, are servants of the Pharoah, and Pharoah the servant of Amon, and Amon the servant of Re, and Re—"

"Yes?" Irun asked curiously.

"The servant of himself, I suppose," said Fl'ret. "And all of us are servants of ourselves and servants of others and I for one would not have it otherwise. A world where everyone was independent, sufficient to herself, neither needing nor giving support—I'd find little comfort there. Now see," she said. "We have arrived too late. The chariot is headed for the stables, which means your parents have arrived and gone to their quarters. This is what comes of so much talk."

Irun didn't answer. They were at the great gate in the high wall that surrounded Perub's estate. Grapevines covered the wall as far as she could see, along with espaliered fig trees. The grapes were not the succulent fine grapes of the oases, but a homelier fruit that made a daily table wine. Date palms and dom palms, acacias and tamarisks, pomegranate and persea trees filtered the fierce sunlight that seemed to shine with steady and undiminished brilliance all day, to be eclipsed by sudden swift twilight at evening. Around the corner, out of sight, Irun knew there were many outbuildings—the stables, the bakery and kitchens, the storerooms and granary, the linen shed and wine cellar. And beyond would be the large garden where fruits and vegetables were grown. It pleased her that she knew all this, could picture all those places. And other buildings were there, also. Quarters for her father's many servants and—for his slaves.

Slaves?

Irun frowned. "How can a person keep slaves?" she said to Fl'ret, ignoring the woman's impatient gesture. "Does that seem right to you, Fl'ret? For a person to *own* other people?"

"We must get back," Fl'ret urged. "Your parents will be eager to see you."

"My father will be," said Irun. "The man who keeps slaves—he'll be glad to see me."

"Little goose—"

"I asked you something, Fl'ret."

"Well then, small imperiousness, your father cannot very well tell Pharoah to take his gift and toss it to the Nile crocodile. None but Ayu and El-oy are slaves here, and they were a gift of the old Pharoah to your father, who could only express gratitude and accept. When El-oy is older, she will be freed."

"And Ayu?"

"Ayu's wits wander. He would not be safe as a freed man, if he took a mind to go out on his own in the world. He would most certainly be waylaid or done ill in some way, and would not have sense to protect himself. Your father is Ayu's protection. Now, will you please come back to your room, where your parents can find you when they send for you?"

They turned toward the women's quarters, Irun lingering by the pool to watch the golden fish meander beneath floating lotus blossoms.

Fl'ret went off with a shrug that clearly said she'd done her best with a stubborn donkey of a girl and now she was going to see to her own person, getting it ready to greet the master and the mistress when they called her.

Irun smiled and sat down at the pool's edge, dangling her bare legs in the water. She found that if she stayed very still the curious carp would approach and at length delicately nibble at her toes. She sighed deeply, alone for the first time in—in how long? She could not remember when she'd last been alone or where that had been. Her head seemed to be detached, floating a little distance away from her, and her vision was misty. It was not unpleasing, this sensation.

I am Irun, daughter of Perub and Bel.

Erin, came a faint echo in her head. *Daughter of Peter and—*

No, no, no—I am Irun. *Irun.*

I am Irun, possessed by a demon, and the demon's name is *Erin.* She outwitted the beetle mixture and the Governor's physician, but she's not going to outwit me. I'll keep her inside, and settle down to live with her, or outwait her, or do anything at all except see the doctor again. I don't want to die yet. She was too young, she was sure, to die. But if the doctor forced her to swallow a chopped-up mouse she'd surely die immediately afterward. And if he tried to get her to swallow a live mouse, she'd die first.

Maybe, she thought, I could get accustomed to sharing myself with a demon. Get used to being dizzy. Maybe I could even get to like it, after a time. Maybe—

"Irun, my little floating leaf, my little river ibis, here am I, your father!"

Irun scrambled to her feet and ran into the arms of the stocky, dark, and handsome man approaching. Held in his arms, against the deep chest, so close she could feel the thumping of his wonderful heart, Irun felt, for the first time that she could remember at all, safe. Quite safe.

"Come," he said. "Let us sit by the pool and talk."

"But you're covered with dust, and you must be tired." Say that doesn't matter. Say, oh, *that's* nothing, I'll stay with you for a while anyway.

"That's all right," said Perub. "I'll go and bathe presently. But since I've been dusted liberally by that abominable red desert sand blowing onto the river for many many miles, a little while longer won't matter. Your mother," he added, "is very tired and of course cannot wait for her bath. We wondered that you did not meet us at the gate."

"We went, but we got there too late."

"And have you been well?"

"Oh, yes! Very *very* well."

"You speak with much emphasis. Does that mean you have not been well?"

"No, father. It means—I've been well. And now that you're back, I am very very well." Maybe she could still persuade Fl'ret to keep silent, persuade Fl'ret that there was no need to— But there was the matter of the bill of the Governor's physician. He would expect at least a brace of fine geese. Oh, well, let Fl'ret tell about it. For the moment, she just wanted to enjoy being with her father. How long had he been gone? No matter how she tried, she could not remember.

Perub looked at her reflectively, but in a moment went on, "I have brought you a present."

"You have? What is it? Where is it? Your hands are empty. Did you buy me something too big to carry?"

"I shall not tell you what, but I'll tell you where. It will be here tomorrow when the barge arrives. I put it in the care of Kafa."

Kafa was her father's steward, who went with him everywhere. Kafa would be coming on the barge with

126

the baggage, the kitchen boat following. He would make sure that all was properly cared for and accounted for. If her present was in his care it would be carefully seen to. But what could it be?

"Shall I guess?"

"No, because you might guess correctly and I want to surprise you. Tell me what you have done in my absence."

What had she done? She was frightened to find she could not recall what she'd been doing before Fl'ret had wakened her by the mastaba. Only that brief half-remembered scene outside the Temple School with Edzme and Seti and Fayet and Semary. She swallowed nervously and began, "Well, mostly I—"

Then El-oy, on her soundless feet, was beside them, saying in her almost inaudible voice that Madam was asking for Perub.

"Oh, well," said Perub, getting to his feet. "I knew this wouldn't be a long visit. Coming, Irun?"

Irun shook her head. "She didn't ask for me, only for you."

"Well, but—" Perub rubbed a hand over his grimy cheek, which was beginning to show a beard. "All right, Irun. Just as well perhaps. After such a long journey your mother will be tired."

"Of course."

Too tired, anyway, for me. She looked at her father with woeful eyes and in a sudden gesture he pulled her close again. Irun realized he was trying to comfort her for her mother's indifference without saying anything against Bel herself. Poor Father, she thought. I could tell him I don't care what she thinks of me, but he wouldn't believe it. She knew that when she looked at him with an expression of drowning sadness—an expression which was not entirely artful but which she could, nevertheless, assume at will—he felt overwhelmed with protective and helpless love.

If I were kind, she thought, I wouldn't do this to him. If I were kind I'd love him and be merry and make friends with other children so he wouldn't always see me—see me so neglected and lonely. But if she were merry and indifferent and had a lot of friends, wouldn't her father then just turn to his wife completely?

After he'd gone, Irun wandered around the courtyard, thinking unhappily that all of it was, after all, *her* fault. Bel's. It's in no way *mine*, she said to herself. If *she* loved me or even paid attention to me, then I wouldn't have to spend all this time fighting for my father's attention.

She doesn't give me a *chance* to be like other children, so fond of their parents that they don't have to think about them.

CHAPTER THIRTEEN

On the first night of their return, Perub and Bel retired to their quarters, seeing no one except Fl'ret and Remunun, the household steward, to receive reports of how things had gone in their absence. They took a simple meal and retired early. Bel sent word through Fl'ret that since Irun had not seen fit to greet them at the gate, she would not be summoned into their presence that evening.

Fl'ret tried to make this message sound less chilly when she delivered it as she and Irun prepared for bed.

"Your lady mother is weary from her journey. What she and your father need now is a good night's sleep."

"Did you—tell them?"

Fl'ret hesitated. "No. There did not seem to be a propitious moment."

"That's good," Irun sighed as she lay down on her bed. The room still seemed to swing around, perhaps a little less tumultuously than earlier in the day—as if she'd left an area of cataract and now just floated on the gently heaving body of the river.

In each corner of the room an alabaster oil lamp glowed softly, keeping at a distance night devils who were known to roam the dark with their faces on backward. Above each lamp was a charm inscribed on the wall in the lovely picture writing that Irun longed to understand. She knew what this charm said and sometimes tried to teach herself to draw the figures. *"O Demon or Rejected Spirit, quit this place for it is lighted against you!"*

Irun had been told that poor people could not afford oil to burn a lamp at night. They slept in darkness. She wondered why Pharaoh, with all his riches, did not provide each poor family with a lamp and oil to burn in it. When she had asked this of her father, he'd looked thoughtful but had no answer for her. Perhaps only someone her age would question the ways of the King.

Moonlight coming through the high clerestory windows fell across the frescoed walls, making the colors, so brilliant by day, seem silvery and pale. Hunting wildfowl in the marshes.

She had gone with them a few times, with Perub and *her*, to the marshes. They would take Perub's long papyrus skiff, and when Ayu had poled them toward the center of the marsh, her father would pick up his throw stick and toss it into the flock of ducks or geese that had risen at their approach. He could, on a good day, supply the entire household with wild game to eat. Irun was not one of those who preferred wild birds to the domestic ducks and geese and pigeons grown at home for food, and she did not like to see the struck bird fall. But to be with her father overcame all other objections.

On these trips, Bel would sit beneath a light canopy, fanned by El-oy or some other handmaiden, looking dreamily at the passing scene, indifferently at the stricken birds, and proudly at Perub. At Irun she scarcely looked at all.

She holds me at fault because I'm not graceful and pretty. Or because I'm not a boy. But really that's *her* fault. Hers and—and Perub's. *They* were the sculptors who'd fashioned this image, Irun. Why doesn't she blame her own self for what I am? A beautiful woman who could only produce one child and couldn't make that one either a boy *or* beautiful. *She's* the one at fault.

Erin, stop feeling sorry for yourself—it's so unattractive!

Irun started up, staring around the dimly lighted room. What was that? What had that been? That—that *voice*, that babble of incomprehensible sounds? Had it been a trick of the dark, of her mind, of the fountains purling in the courtyard? Had she spoken *herself*? Not knowing?

She wished that Fl'ret slept somewhere else than here in this room. Because I shall have to fall asleep myself sometime, she thought, and suppose when I slept Fl'ret should wake, and suppose I talked in this mad tongue. She would know then for sure that the demon is still lodged within me. She shuddered, opening her eyes as wide as they'd go.

But after a while her lids fell, and she began to slide toward sleep. Eyes closed, she began to hum. . . .

> Twinkle, twinkle, little bat!
> How I wonder what you're at!
> Up above the world you fly,
> Like a tea tray in the sky. . . .

Fl'ret was shaking her.

"Irun, Irun," she whispered harshly. "Wake up, wake up!"

Irun dragged her eyes open. "Why, Flora?" she asked drowsily. "I'm asleep. Why must I wake up?"

"Because you were singing."

"Singing? In my sleep? How nice. I must be happy."

"Irun, you were singing in that strange language again. And just now you called me *Flora* again. It is not you that knows these sounds. It must be—"

"Hush!" Irun put her hand softly on Fl'ret's lips. "Hush, Fl'ret. Don't tell. Don't tell anybody."

Fl'ret grasped the girl's wrist and lowered her hand. "Can we keep this thing between ourselves? The demon is within you still. Can we keep this from your parents, from your father?"

"It can't be a bad demon," Irun giggled. "Not if it *sings*. What did it say, Fl'ret?"

"I don't know," the woman said slowly. "I *almost* knew. Something about a—a *bat*. And a *tea tray*. What is a *tea*? What is a *tray*? What could you—could *she*—be talking about?"

Irun shook her head. The movement made her wince. My head, she thought, feels as if *it* were on a *tea tray* in the sky. Whirling around up there, like a *bat*. "*Twinkle, twinkle* . . ." You'd think Fl'ret would know what a *tea tray* is. It's a *tray* to put the *tea* things on, for goodness' sakes. Or *cocoa* things, of course . . .

She looked quickly at Fl'ret, to see if she'd spoken aloud. It seemed not. She took Fl'ret's hands in hers. "Please, please let me have a few days to see if the demon will go on her own accord. I cannot take any more of the Governor's physician's medicine magic. If I take any more, I will surely die."

"But suppose he sends his bill, asking for corn or a goose or who knows what. How do I explain that?"

"He won't right *away*, will he? It would look rude to send a bill the moment my father gets home from being on the King's business. I'm sure the Governor's physician wouldn't wish to look *rude*."

"But—"

"I shall *die,* Fl'ret, and go into my coffin with my butterfly pin and my heart scarab and my little shabti of you and nothing else because I haven't had time to get anything else, and *you* will miss me."

"Stop, oh, stop," Fl'ret said miserably. "All right. I shall do as you ask, though I am not sure, not sure at all, that what you ask is right. I shall wait three days and four nights, and if by then the demon has not flown—giving us a sign as she goes—then I shall have to tell the master. And he will beat me for having kept it from him so long," she grumbled.

Irun laughed. "Beat you, Fl'ret? Perub?"

"He will be angry."

"People get angry, and they get over being angry."

"Well, then—go to sleep." Fl'ret put her hand on Irun's forehead. "Go to sleep, little bird."

Strange, Irun thought, as she drifted off again, strange that if *some* people call you a bird, or a little ibis, they say it with love and mean that you are—

well, no one would call me *pretty*—but they say it meaning they find me someone to love, maybe someone lovely, which isn't the same as pretty. But if other people say the same thing, like Fayet and Semary calling me ibis-headed and saying I wanted to be Thoth— why *they* are just being mean.

Seti was nice, though. He tried to stop them from jeering at me because I said that a girl had as much right to learn as a boy did.

She put her arm over her eyes. No wonder they'd laughed. Where did she *get* such ideas?

If from my demon then she's not a stupid one. Only peculiar, with strange notions.

She wondered if she could somehow pretend to Fl'ret that the demon had taken flight. Do something—perhaps fall to the ground and froth?—that would persuade Fl'ret the exodus had taken place. Then she could settle down to live with this weird spirit, who might prove better company than the girls she knew now.

I must try, she told herself. Even if she had to go through the rest of her life with her head spinning, it might be worth it to keep the demon and ward off the doctor.

And what about her poor ka-t, her true spirit, out there wandering homeless, bodiless? She must lure it back. If she relaxed and was *very* welcoming, perhaps it would come in and nestle with the demon, and the three of them could press on together. . . .

She was weary, very weary. She was—

For the second time that night she fell asleep and this time neither dreamed nor sang.

CHAPTER FOURTEEN

The evening before, when Perub had returned from his long trip to the Greater Oasis, he had been wearing his black curling wig, a long linen robe, his heavy chain of office around his neck, armlets, rings, and leather scandals. So attired, even layered with grime and dust, he was an impressive, rather awesome figure.

The next morning, wearing a white cotton kilt, face and head closely shaven, brown and bounding as a young lion, he set the household thrumming like a plucked harp string. Still impressive, Irun thought. But not a man who sought to awe.

"It's never like this when Father is away," she said to Fl'ret, who was attempting to pull down some of the short hair over her left cheek so as to make a side curl. "Ow, Fl'ret. Stop! That hurts."

"Well, we shall have to use the ringlet again."

Irun shot toward the door as Fl'ret reached toward

the inlaid chest. She turned at the beaded curtain. "I don't have to wear it during the day, do I?"

Fl'ret shrugged good-humoredly. "I suppose not."

Still Irun lingered. "Keep your promise, now."

"I always do."

"Of course. Well—" Her father's voice came nearer. "I must go."

"Re keep you."

Fl'ret will keep her promise, Irun thought. Only *I* will—could—give myself away. Because her father, whether redoubtable in his robes of office or relaxed in his informal home attire, was keen. He would not long miss something amiss in his daughter.

"Well then," he said now, as they met in the courtyard. "Would you like to spend the morning with me?"

"Oh, yes. Yes, I would."

"I have many things to do, but I can fit you in as we go along," he said, smiling. "First, we had best go to your mother, who is eager to see her daughter after many days' separation." His voice was bland as he said this, and Irun made no protest. It was simpler this way. With relations between *her* and herself unexplained, they could pretend there wasn't anything to be explained.

The quarters her parents shared were spacious and luxurious, with large cushions scattered on the floor and the floor itself designed to look like a riverbed with fishes and plants brightly painted. Here and there were rush rugs dyed yellow and carnelian and cornflower blue. On the walls, painted columns with lotus tops seemed to support the ceiling, and between the columns and across the ceiling were murals of wild animals and birds. Her parents' chairs were roomy, of ebony and ivory inlaid with gold leaf, and there were other smaller chairs with rush seats and faïence inlays. In one corner a great alabaster jar was filled with water and covered with leaves to keep the water cool and insect-free. Through high windows the sunlight came, pleasantly filtered by nearly opaque glass. Their great bed was on a brick dais against the wall, and it, too, was of ebony and ivory with a thick linen mesh mattress. The legs ended in ducks' heads, perfectly carved and painted so that their eyes seemed to stare across the room.

The Vizier's mansion was much grander than this estate of Perub's, and of course the Pharaoh's palace, to which she had been once with her father, was beyond compare. Yet this room seemed, to Irun, to be the most beautiful she had ever seen. And she—her mother—the most beautiful woman she had ever seen, with hair and eyes as black as sloes and long neck held so proudly.

Lying on the floor beside her, his head pushing against her carelessly caressing palm, was a leopard. When Bel was home, he was with her—silent, beautiful, envied by her friends. He had been given to her, a spitting squirming kitten, by the old Pharaoh. The leopard, now grown, was named Ta-ka-lo.

Irun found him the saddest creature she had ever known. She tried not to look at him, not to think of him. Deprived of his sex, his claws, and his upper fangs, he seemed to her as lost, as aimless and rudderless, as those spirits of the rejected dead that roam the night searching for peace, for a body to inhabit. But where the spirits were sometimes vengeful, there seemed not to be even bitterness in Ta-ka-lo's eyes. Those great cat orbs, which should have glowed like coals, looked out on the world with no expression at all. Docile, disarmed, mentally clouded, he followed Bel when she was home and lay, dully patient, waiting, when she was not.

Irun could remember when he had first had his claws removed, when he'd been a kitten. He had not been able to understand what had happened. He continued to try to dash up trees out of bounding high spirits and repeatedly fell to the ground, sprawling and bewildered. He'd attempt to run across the courtyard to greet Bel, but getting no purchase on the floor would slide sideways, or forward—landing on his chin, his legs splayed. She could remember that some people had laughed at his clumsy behavior. Bel never laughed. She would gather him to her, and croon in his ear, and press his head against her breast, comforting him. "Poor Ta-ka-lo," she'd mourn. "Poor beauty. Try to understand that it is for your own good I have to have these things done to you. So that you would never grow up fierce and savage and have to be taken from me. Poor love, poor beauty."

"But it isn't for his own good!" Irun stormed one day to her father. "It's because she wanted to keep him and the only way she could keep him was to *ruin* him. For his own good he should have been put back in the bush when he was grown! For his own good he'd have been better *killed*!"

Perub, who never listened to criticism of Bel, had turned away without comment, even though Irun knew—*knew*—that he agreed with her.

Now her gaze slid over the gorgeous demoralized beast to the woman in the chair. She said, "I hope you had a good trip."

"Exhausting, my poppy. Utterly. But the opportunity to be with your father made the rigors of the voyage tolerable."

Irun thought of her father's exquisitely appointed boat, and of the barge and kitchen boat following. Rigorous! She thought, You have all the opportunities you wish to be with him. She said dutifully, "It is good to have you home again."

"How nice." Bel's eyes widened. "Where is your side curl, Irun?"

Irun clapped a hand to her left ear. She might have known, should certainly have known, that her mother would notice the missing curl. She should have had an explanation ready. "I—I cut it accidentally."

"How could you accidentally cut your side curl off?"

"I was—I was trying to trim my hair with the razor, and it—it just accidentally came off."

"Come closer."

Irun sidled across the room. She smiled at Ani, who was plaiting Bel's hair. There was no help from that quarter. Ani looked at a cluster of cornflowers painted near the ceiling. Irun glanced back to catch her father's eye. He was no longer there. She could hear his voice in the courtyard, inquiring of Ayu whether the barge with the baggage donkeys had been sighted yet, coming up the Nile.

"There is no use trying to avoid me, Irun," said Bel. "Come over here so that I can look at you. And do straighten up. *Must* you walk hunched over like a scribe at his papyrus roll? Have you ever noticed how *tall* the Vizier's daughters walk, how graceful they look? Wouldn't you like—"

Irun, inspired, said, "One of them ran away with a Syrian."

It worked. Absolutely, decisively. Side curl forgotten, Bel stared at her daughter. "Are you mad? What are you *saying*? One of the Vizier's daughters and a—a *Syrian*? She would never be allowed back in her father's house."

"I guess she doesn't want to be allowed back. She went to Syria with him. He had a beard."

"*A beard*! One of the Vizier's daughters has left our country, this country, *the* only civilized or inhabitable or beautiful country on the face of the earth, to run off with a Syrian with a beard and live in another land?" Bel was fluttering with excitement. "Is this true, Ani?" she demanded of her maid.

"Yes, Madam."

"Why I—why I—why, I simply do not know what to say." She laid a finger against her cheek, frowned exquisitely, brooded a moment, pushing Ta-ka-lo's thrusting head aside.

"To leave our land with a bearded barbarian—"

"Maybe he isn't a barbarian. Maybe—"

"Don't be witless. Of course he's a barbarian. All people except us, *The* People, are barbarians."

Irun decided not to argue. She was content to have had this sudden recollection that took attention away from her side curl. Besides, no one ever argued with Bel. She was too sincerely incapable of grasping a point of view other than her own.

"Which one?" she said suddenly.

"Bref-ni."

"The eldest! The loveliest! Why, she is a—*was*—a priestess of Amon!"

Lovely Bref-ni had been, indeed, a priestess, entitled to dance in the Outer Temple (only men, of course, ever penetrated to the Inner Temple, and only priests to the Inner Sanctum) and rattle the sistrum on feast days. Bref-ni's sistrum had been exquisite. A bronze hoop, strung with wires threaded with metal discs and mounted on an ivory handle carved with the head of Hathor, the Cow Goddess. It had a vibrant, twanging sound, the sistrum, when shaken by the priestesses of Amon doing the slow ritual dance at the Festival of Amon. Irun couldn't see how Bref-ni had brought herself to relinquish this great honor. Especially as priestesses were permitted to learn a little of the great hieroglyphic writing. She wondered if Bref-ni had taken her sistrum and her jewels with her when she fled.

Like Bel, Irun could not understand how anyone could leave this perfect land. Certainly not to run away with a man with a beard and one who, more-over, had his own hair, and a lot of it, on his head. Surely such a mess of hair would smell and have—*things*—in it? How could Bref-ni have grown up know-ing the smooth brown shaven heads of Egyptian men and then run off with a hairy Syrian merchant? Still, it was a fact that she had.

"My robe, Ani," said Bel. "And ask Ayu to bring round my carrying chair. He and—well, tell him to get somebody—they can carry me round to the Governor's mansion, where I can find out what has been going on in my absence. Great Isis! What scandal!" she said happily.

"May I go now?"

"What? Oh, yes, yes, of course. We shall be having a party in a few nights, my poppy, and you may at-tend." Momentarily her thoughts reverted to the prob-lem of the curl. "Perhaps Fl'ret can find you a lock."

"She already has."

"Well, good. Although I still fail to see—well, let it go. Ani, will you run along and fetch Ayu? What are you waiting for? The morning is almost *gone*." She looked at Irun. "You might have told me this sooner."

"I wasn't here sooner."

"Ta-ka-lo, *will* you leave me *alone*. Poor beast," she said, relenting, and absently stroked his head with one hand while with the other she picked up a mirror to study her reflection.

Irun ran from the room and joined her father in the courtyard.

"Why is your mother so overwrought?" Perub asked. "I could hear her voice all the way out here. Have you two got into a disagreement already?" he asked, forgetting to pretend that Irun and Bel never disagreed.

"Not this time. I was telling her that Bref-ni, the Vizier's daughter, ran away with a Syrian merchant while you were in the desert."

Perub gasped. "Is this true?"

"Why do people ask me if something is true when I say it. How could I make *up* such a thing? Why would I?"

"True, true. Forgive me, Irun. I spoke out of astonishment, not disbelief. Osiris! What a scandal! How is the city taking it? What are people saying?"

"I don't know. I was—" She broke off before she could confess that for a while she'd had no memory of anything. Now that things were coming back to her, surely she was being cured? "I wasn't told much. Fl'ret doesn't think I should know about things like that."

"Things like that! There's never been anything *else* like it." Perub shook his head. "Piankhy will be either sick to the death or in such a rage that no one will dare approach him. Perhaps he'll go after her," he mused. "Although how he could bring her back—"

"The Vizier and his wife say that they never had a daughter named Bref-ni. Wherever her name occurs in their tomb it is being chipped away or painted out, and no one is to say it again. Her name. I heard that much from Fayet and Semary—they were talking about it all over the nome. Bref-ni is as if she had never been. Sen'ti is now the eldest of the daughters, and she is to be the priestess of Amon, and rattle the sistrum, and learn to read a little. If it isn't too late for her to learn. Father, maybe one day I could—"

"I wonder what the King says." It was so unusual for him to interrupt that Irun felt tears start to her eyes. Why isn't somebody interested in *me*? she thought. Who cares if Bref-ni ran away with a bristly merchant? She could run away with a hippopotamus for all I care.

"Pharaoh has forgiven the Vizier," she said sulkily. "Semary told that much, too. She and Fayet think it's very exciting and they don't miss Bref-ni at all. She ordered them around all the time and told their secrets if they were dumb enough to let her find them out—Fayet and Semary are pretty dumb. And she sometimes pinched or slapped them and then said she hadn't when they complained to the Vizier, and of course he believed Bref-ni because she was his favorite. That's why nobody's ever to mention her again, I suppose," Irun said reflectively. "It would make his heart ache to hear her name."

Perub looked down at his daughter and smiled gently. "What a wise little ibis it is." He slapped his hands together, as if dismissing one line of thought before taking up another. "What do you say, Irun. Shall we walk to the quayside or take the light chariot?"

"I'd far rather walk," Irun said eagerly. "Walking through the town—oh, I'd love that."

"Then let's go quickly before your mother knows what we're up to. She'd insist at least on carrying chairs. She'd think I—that is, we—would not be safe on foot."

"Why shouldn't we be safe?"

"We should be. Shall be. Your mother is a worrier. She thinks footpads and scoundrels lie in wait for anyone who steps outside the wall unprotected."

CHAPTER FIFTEEN

They strolled toward the town on the sandy road, the hot white sun beating on their brown and nearly naked bodies. All around them the industry of day went on—diligent, clamorous, unceasing, in ancient, changeless patterns. A herdsman drove his cattle past, stirring up a cloud of sand and dust. He bowed low in passing them, nearly touching his forehead to the ground. In the fields, farmers filled the irrigation ditches by means of wooden shadufs—buckets on counterpoised poles that dipped into canals, filled, lifted. The precious water was tipped into a ditch, the bucket descended again, filled, lifted. Year in, year out, the length of the Nile, men worked the shadufs from sunup to sundown.

Now, in autumn, when the great brown river, their Nilus, had receded, leaving behind the rich black mud in which nearly any crop would grow, the farmers prepared the fields for sowing and planting. Seeds were trodden into the soft earth by sheep and pigs, and soon emmer wheat and barley and flax would cover the land. Papyrus would grow wild in the marshes and along the banks of the river. Already the estates of noblemen were producing vegetables and fruit. Their gardens were enriched over the years by layers of Nile mud brought in wagons to their dwelling places, situated well back from any threat of flooding should the river rise to high. This had been a good Nile year, with the godlike Hapi rising just enough to make a perfect harvest, but not so much that the houses and shops of poor people, built not far enough above the dykes, would be flooded or even washed away.

Irun knew from Fl'ret and Kafa that the poor ate mostly beans and lentils. They fished, since the Nile opened her breast to all. But they rarely had meat, since they could not take to the marshes and hunt wildfowl or game. And they did not have gardens in which to grow the beautiful fruits and vegetables enjoyed by the wealthy.

"Why should some people be poor and some be rich?" Irun asked.

Perub said flatly, "That I cannot answer. I have pondered the question and concluded it cannot be answered, not even by the gods. It is as it is. The sun consumes himself in the evening, renews himself each morning, like the phoenix. The river rises and recedes. A man is born and he dies. Some have riches and some live in poverty. It is as it is."

"But something could be *done* about rich and poor," Irun persisted. "It isn't like the sun or the river. It's—*things*. Clothes, food. We could divide everything up, couldn't we? Giving each person just as much as another person has. Just the same amount of garden, the same number of pieces of jewelry, the same number of chairs—"

"And shortly we'd find some men living in houses behind walls with large gardens and any number of chairs, and some men living in huts and eating lentils."

"But why?"

"I cannot answer that," Perub repeated.

Irun supposed that if Perub couldn't then he was right, even the gods would have no answer.

"If *I* were Pharaoh," she began, and stopped at a glance from her father. "Just the same—" she tried again, and again was stopped without a word.

But what a strange world it was, where you couldn't even *question* things. It had always been that way, of course. She wondered if it would always, forever, be so. One day, thousands of moons from now, would a good man like her father still ponder why some people could glut themselves their whole lives long, while others went to sleep hungry every night of their lives, and conclude, as her father did now, that "It is as it is"?

Along the waterfront, as they came to town, were great storehouses, wharfs, and landing stages, and the Customs House. The river swarmed with ships, the shore with people and animals. Noisy, smelly, exciting. Beer houses rang with the laughter and growls of sailors, the smell of food cooking on braziers over beds of glowing charcoal filled the nostrils deliciously—strong and spicy it was, though Perub sniffed fastidiously and turned his head a little as they passed a pig turning on a spit. Irun couldn't see that it smelled different than a pig being roasted in the great kitchen at home. She found the odor of bread and beer and roasting pig pungent and stimulating, and found poignant the sound of an invisible musician playing a reedy tune somewhere in the marketplace. Everything everywhere was accompanied by the braying of donkeys hard at work.

"O Great Bes," said Perub, "here comes Piankhy with a face like a sandstorm. Irun, go amuse yourself in the marketplace and meet me at our landing stage. I shall try not to be long with the Vizier, so do not linger."

Irun needed no urging to absent herself from the Vizier's presence. She shot into the anonymity of the marketplace as Piankhy bore down upon her father.

In there the noise was exhilarating, and she soon found the musician, who was sitting with his back against a potter's stall, piping to attract the attention of passers-by. Irun watched as the potter, driving his heavy wheel with his right leg, seemed to lift a vase like a veil with his deft fingers. The wheel turned and the lump of clay took shape sinuously under the direction of steady hands that had fashioned, Irun supposed, hundreds, maybe thousands, of cups and bowls and vases and would perhaps shape thousands more. The potter looked to be an old man, but a strong and healthy old man. She had a sudden recollection of another old man, the Pharaoh who had died long ago, when she had been a very little girl. He, too, had been a strong man—only driven to madness with the pain in his teeth. It was said that he had drunk himself to death, trying to escape the torment. This potter did not look as though his teeth troubled him. Irun smiled at the flute player and moved on.

The row of stalls she ambled by was overseen by the King's bodyguard, because the craftsmen here were working in fine materials—leather for sandals, linen for cushions and robes and hangings, gold for jewelry. The bodyguards stood at attention, discouraging activity on the part of the light-fingered. She passed a sandalmaker, a harnessmaker, a cabinetmaker, stopped briefly to watch a jeweler at work. He sat cross-legged at the door to his stall, carving a scarab in red jasper. Behind him were displayed examples of his work. Pendants hanging from braided cord, from thin gold chains. Bracelets and earrings and armlets and anklets. Bright beads strung on wire. Finger rings, collars. One of his collars, of gold with insets of flowers formed from green feldspar and lapis lazuli and carnelian, was so pretty that Irun drew in her breath.

"Would you like to have that?" Perub asked, appearing suddenly beside her.

"Oh, no. I don't want two presents. Shall I guess yet what Kafa is bringing?"

"No, no, no," said Perub as they walked on. "Do not even remember that he is bringing you something. Be totally taken by surprise."

Irun smiled. "What did the Vizier want?"

"I'm not sure. I'm not sure he wanted anything except his daughter back."

"Did he say anything about her?"

"No. I doubt he ever will. But he has a headache and a bellyache, and I am sure, a heartache. So he talked with me about the wine harvest. A man can always put his mind to business and so drive out other matters. For a while, for a while."

He was walking very fast and Irun had to run to keep up. Running made her head spin. Perhaps after all she should have asked to ride in the light chariot.

Trying to keep the muddled condition of her mind from people's notice, trying to conceal not only lapses in memory, but the presence of memories that had no place in her life—it all had her hard-pressed, enmeshed in difficulties.

"*Gandy!*" she exclaimed, and her hand in her father's tightened.

"What's that?"

"I—*Gandy . . . gandy*. It's a word."

"No word I ever heard. What does it mean?"

"I don't know. Does it mean anything to you, Father?"

"No, not that I—no, no. It's not familiar to me. Where did you hear it?"

With an effort, Irun kept herself from flinging at him the whole tale of what had been going on with her since she'd wakened in the shadow of the mastaba, plagued with headache, dizziness, and the presence of recollections and a language in her mind that had no place there. What a relief, what a relaxing, joy-giving relief it would be to tell her father and let him take over the burden and apprehension that now she and Fl'ret had to share. But the memory of the gaunt, fell physician-magician and his sack of cures stopped her tongue and she said, "I'm not sure. It's just a word I heard. That's all."

When she was alone, later today sometime, she'd have to take this word *gandy* and try to work it out, fit it in. *Gandy*. It felt desperately important, like something that should have much bearing on her life, and yet she could not find a place to work it in.

They were at the docks now, and as they walked to Perub's landing stage to wait for a sight of his towing boat with the barge behind it, Irun looked at the broad brown river and felt, all at once, quite peaceful.

Yes, it had been a good Nile year. The river rising, with its annual largesse of life-giving soil, to just the right height, flooding the fields but not the town. Now it had returned to its deep bed, having done its job of fertilizing the earth. For months to come it would bear along its great length all the traffic of Egypt. There were ships out there now, Irun knew, making their way up-river on expeditions to Nubia to mine for bronze and silver and the beautiful lapis lazuli. Ships bound in the other direction to the great green sea above the Delta and so on up to Macedonia and Lebanon and Syria, where Egyptian merchants would barter gold for timber and for spices. The river resounded with the shouts of captains, chants of rowers, the creak of rigging. Barges went by in tow, lying low in the water with heavy cargo—produce, cattle, granite for tombs and temples.

Across the water, on the western bank, a funeral train could be seen pulling up to shore. In the lead, a slender, black, high-prowed boat bore the Osiris himself, lying amidships beneath a canopy. Behind that came a second boat, laden with the possessions of the dead man that he was taking with him to his tomb in the western hills. In a third boat came the family. They were being met by hired professional mourners who were already beating their breasts and wailing.

"In the next world," Irun said, settling beside her father on the landing stage, "everything will be as it is here, only better?"

"Indeed it will be."

"And we'll all be happy and reunited and possessed of all the things we have here?"

"All we can take with us."

"Then why do we wail for the dead? If everything's going to be so wonderful and go on forever, why cry and carry on when somebody sets forth?"

"You're in a questioning mood today."

Irun nodded.

"Possibly," said Perub, "even knowing, as we do know, that all will go on as it always has, we still—because *we* are here yet and someone we love has gone before—think of ourselves, instead of celebrating his happy state."

"Or hers."

"Of course. Instead of thinking of their felicity, we only realize that we ourselves are for the time being bereft. And so we are sad and wail for our loss."

"Father," said Irun, feeling close and warm and secure with him, and so daring to speak of things she would not mention at home, "are you not frightened at having only me, a daughter, for your child? No son, to be your Horus when you have gone West, to bring offerings for your ka? I know that only a male child can be a Horus. A son, with acceptable offerings and prayers, could see that the ka-priests remembered his father, and his father's father and so back forever. But a daughter?"

"Make your mind easy on that score," said Perub with a grave smile. "I have worked it all out to my total satisfaction. I had meant to speak to you of this when you grew older, but since you yourself have brought the matter up, let me tell you that I have decided *you* shall be my Horus."

Irun felt a wave of almost intolerable joy, and following on it a rush of terror at the realization that her father could, one day would, actually die.

"Are you all right, Irun?" he asked sharply. "What's wrong?"

Entirely forgetful of her own problems, Irun grasped his hand and said, "Father, promise me you will not leave me for many years to come, that I shall not be your Horus until—until you and I are both old, very very anciently *old*. Promise me!"

Perub looked at her a long time before he said, "I promise that I shall try in every way to do as you ask. That is the most I can promise."

She closed her eyes, opened them, and nodded. It was, of course, all he could promise.

"Why, Irun," he said gently. "Just now you said that we should not weep for the one who goes forth first."

"It doesn't matter what I said. I am frightened. Of losing you, mostly. But of lots of things."

"Like what?"

"Oh—of *real* things. Like the spirits of the unworthy dead who wander in the night with their faces on backward."

Perub laughed. "You consider that one of the *real* things."

Confused, Irun said, "Don't you believe that the rejected spirits wander the earth, looking for a home in someone's body?"

"I find it difficult to believe, let us say that."

"Then—if not that—how can you believe in all the rest? In the Court of Osiris, and the Isles of Bliss, and the Fields of Offerings? If you don't believe in the spirits how can you believe in eternal life?"

"I'm selective in my beliefs, little ibis. I feel—" He paused to reflect. "I believe in Eternal Life, and in Osiris, and in the greatness of Re. I think I do not put much credence in demons."

But *I* have a demon inside me, Irun wanted to shout at him. Your daughter beside you is *possessed*!

She clenched her teeth, holding the words back.

Perub, however, was staring across the river at the funeral procession, now winding its way up into the hills, the dead man and his wealth being dragged on sleds, the priests and family and mourners following after. It was the funeral of one of the wealthiest merchants of the nome, whose body had been in preparation seventy days for this, the day of his burial. Even a Pharaoh's body took no longer.

"I remember him," Perub murmured. "I've seen more expression, and more affection, in the eye of a goose than I ever saw in the eyes of that one."

"Will he be judged worthy?"

"Oh, I expect so," Perub said carelessly. "He's very rich."

"Is *that* how Osiris judges?"

Perub moved uneasily. "How you do question, Irun. No, that is not the whole tale. I fear it forms a part. That fellow will arrive at the Court of Judgement with a very long expensive scroll stating that he never did evil against any man or woman, and the scroll will of course have to be taken into account."

"Even if what is said on it isn't true?"

"I said it will be a *very* long one. Who are we to say if *nothing* in it is true, or how much is true? That is for Osiris and Isis and Anubis and Thoth and the forty-two judges to say. Perhaps the man *tried* not to do evil, and perhaps that is sufficient to see him into eternal life."

"But what if a person is poor and can't have a long scroll or even a short scroll drawn up to take with him, testifying to all that stuff? And suppose he really never did do evil? What happens to him? Do you think he isn't worthy of the Isles of Bliss because he can't afford to pay a scribe to write out a scroll *saying* he's worthy?"

"I am a respecter of all persons," Perub said sternly, and Irun dropped her glance. It was true. Her father accorded the same consideration to Ayu as he did to the Vizier. He had, of course, more in common with the Vizier, both of them being men of learning and wealth, but her father's courtesy, his observance of each person as that person and no other, was well known.

"Just the same," she persisted, "if a person can't have an embalmer prepare him for seventy days, and can't take loaves and beer and servants and chairs and jewelry and boats and all the other things he'll need in the next world, and can't bring a scroll saying he's done kindness and nothing else on earth, then how does he get accorded eternal life?"

"If he's been a good man, he will automatically be judged worthy."

"But if he's a rich man, then it doesn't matter whether he's been good?"

"By Amon-Re, you'd call everything into question!" But Perub did not sound annoyed. Rather, he seemed proud of her, interested that she should be talking with him in this manner. "You will make me a fine Horus," he said.

Irun wriggled with pleasure. "How are we going to do it?"

"Well—now, you recall when I took you to the beautiful temple of Hatshepsut?" Irun nodded. "And how I told you that long ago, when he who later became Tuthmosis III was just a child, Hatshepsut ruled the

155

land, first as his regent, and then, feeling she had a right to the throne, by assuming the title of King? Not Queen. King. She ruled as Pharaoh for twenty years, wearing masculine dress and the double crown of Upper and Lower Egypt, and even a false beard for ceremonial occasions. You remember all that?"

Irun nodded.

"My scheme is this, that when I die— Don't shudder," he said, putting his arm over her shoulder. "It will not, I feel confident, be for many many years yet. I love this life too well to hasten to the next one, no matter how felicitous it promises to be. Nevertheless, we must make plans.

"Now, when the time comes—then you will come to my tomb at the appropriate times with a ka-priest of high standing, and you will leave offerings and say prayers for my spirit. You will wear a man's robe and a false beard, and you will point out my many *excellent* qualities, praise me at length—"

"That part will be easy. Do you think we can get away with it? Will the gods and your ka be taken in?"

"My ka will be privy to the facts. And if the offerings are sufficiently lavish I expect the gods will not lift your beard to see the girl's chin underneath."

Irun had a distinct feeling that her father at times was making fun of the gods, but knew that if she questioned him on this directly he would retreat into sternness and reprimand her for impiety.

"You know," she mused, "I have heard it said that sometimes after a person dies he starts all over again working his way up to being a human being." Perub nodded absently. He was searching the river for the sight of his towing boat and barge. "I've heard that a man can die and start out new being an insect, and then work up through birds and animals and so to being a man—or a woman—again. And that it all takes about three thousand years. Have you ever heard of that?"

Perub nodded again. "It's a theory."

"Do you believe in it?"

"I'm prepared to believe in almost any theory."

"But how can you believe that we die and go to the Court of Judgement and then to the Isles of Bliss, if we're worthy, and also think that maybe we begin working our way back up to human shape starting with insects. How can you believe *both*?"

"I *can* believe both, that is all," Perub said tartly. "I can believe a good many things besides, not all of them according with one another."

"But how—"

"I'll put it thus: Our civilization has endured for millenia, and we are a conservative people. We do not readily discard old beliefs just because new ones happen to come along. We embrace them all," he said, lifting his arms in an embracing gesture.

"*Like believing six impossible things before breakfast.*"

"What did you say?"

"When?"

"Just now. What you said just now, I did not catch the words."

Irun shook her head. "I was only asking about your beliefs—"

"No, no. Not then. Just now, a second ago. You spoke a tongue I have never heard." His attention was now all upon her, the river forgotten. "Do it again," he commanded.

"But I can't," Irun said, frightened. "I—"

Oh, *tell him*, she thought. Tell him that a creature from another age, another world, is lodged within you. Tell him, and maybe then your mind will come together again as one, you will be at home here where you belong. "I—" She advanced to the verge of confession, again retreated in horror from the recollection of the physician-magician. Fl'ret had given her three days and four nights. One night and almost a day were past. If in three more nights she did not find her head clear and steady, if she was still saying words in a tongue baffling to her hearers—baffling, indeed, to herself, since she could not summon it at will but found herself speaking it without forewarning—then she would tell her father. Who would most assuredly call the doctor.

O Bes, she thought, calling on her favorite god, next, of course, to Bastet, the Cat Goddess. O Bes, you homely, bandy-legged, laughing, funny god, inspire me to say the right thing! Help me, Bes, adorable laugher!

"It's a language I make up," she blurted, and sighed with relief. How simple. How easy. Why hadn't she thought to say this to Fl'ret? Everyone knew how notional she was. To make up a peculiar language would not be odd in her. She hadn't thought of it because she hadn't thought to call on Bes before, that was why. How stupid of her.

"You make up all those syllables?" Perub said, sounding impressed.

Irun nodded. "I can't always do it. Especially not if somebody asks me to, the way you did, as if you were angry."

"I wasn't angry. I was alarmed. The two emotions

158

tend to sound alike when given voice. So you've made up a language for yourself. How bright you are."

"But that's why I want to go to school, Father. I want to learn to read and write. Fayet and Semary and Edzme laugh at me about it, but Fayet and Semary only want to mince around and giggle and wheedle jewelry from their father, and Edzme hates learning. He'd rather play or hunt than sit in the Scribe's School, learning all the wonderful things he's taught there. *Why* can't a girl be taught something besides how to dance and shake a sistrum?"

"I do not know why, except that it's so rarely done."

"Is that a *reason?*"

"Oh, yes. One of the best. A society does not flourish on new ideas. It rests on old ones."

"I think that is—an abomination."

"You may be right, my infinitely surprising daughter. Of course, priestesses learn to do some reading. Not writing. Bref-ni, for instance—amazing about her, is it not?" he broke off.

But Irun brushed impatiently past the scandalous behavior of Bref-ni. "I'll wager Hatshepsut knew how to read and write."

"You're planning to be King?"

"I'm planning to be your Horus. That's more important. And how will I be able to say the prayers at your tomb if I can't read them?"

Perub nodded thoughtfully. "You could memorize them, perhaps?"

"I'm not *that* bright. There are scrolls and scrolls of prayers. Nobody, not even a priest, could memorize them all. And I'll want you to have them *all* read for your ka," she added.

"Crafty," said Perub. "Full of guile and persuasion. Let me think about this, Irun."

"When you're through thinking, shall I be taught to read and write?"

"I shouldn't be surprised. There is something unusual in you. Not an ordinary girl at all. Now, a tutor, perhaps. At home. I've never heard of its being done, but just the same—"

He leaped to his feet. "There it comes!"

CHAPTER SIXTEEN

Perub's towing boat, pulling the barge, made its way through crowded river traffic to the landing stage. Behind came the kitchen boat. Both had dropped their great square sails some time back, and the rowers were pulling hard at the oars, looking with greedy eyes at the shoreline where they would find beer and their families and rest after the long voyage from the Greater Oasis across the red dry desert and then upriver from Abydos. They were tired and thirsty and longing for women, for the noise and comfort of their families, some of whom crowded the landing stage to greet them. But even as they shipped their oars, all knew that work in plenty lay before them.

Kafa, carrying a whip that he scarcely ever used since he had no need of it, his brawny height and watchful eye being all the exhortation he required, stepped off the boat and bowed to Perub.

"As you see, Master. Here we are."

Perub grasped his servant by both arms. *"Thanks*

be to Re who lights the two lands, and to Sobek, who has brought you safely on the water! No mishaps, Kafa?"

"None."

"Then let us get the unloading done and these fellows can go off, as they are aching to."

The donkeys, who'd brayed sullenly for days, protesting their confinement to the barge, now found they did not wish to leave. They kicked and bellowed and pulled against the reins, to the amusement of onlookers. But finally they were herded on land and started, under the care of Ayu, who had appeared as if knowing precisely the hour to do so, toward Perub's house, and the sailors set to work washing down barge and towing boat. The men on the kitchen boat unloaded what stores were left in preparation for a thorough cleaning of the craft. Menferi, chief cook of the kitchen boat, though only second cook at the mansion, leaped to the landing stage. Like Kafa, and unlike the rowers, he looked refreshed and unfatigued.

He greeted Perub cheerfully and received a respectful salutation in return.

"All is well?"

"All's well," said Menferi. "We'll make everything shipshape here, and then—" He rubbed his hands together, grinning. "—then I shall go to the town." Menferi was not married, and Irun sometimes wondered if this was part of the reason why he was always in a good humor. He answered to no one except Perub, and if Perub offended him—why, there was many another nobleman in these parts would leap at the chance to have Menferi on his cooking boat.

Now he slapped his brow. "Ah, I had nearly forgotten. The gift for Little Miss!" He leaped back in the boat as Perub, smiling broadly, said to Irun, "Turn your back, small ibis. I wish you to be completely surprised."

Irun, who'd been wishing someone would mention her present, wondered again why it had come upriver with Kafa and Menferi rather than on her father's small swift boat that had outdistanced theirs by more than a day. Was it something enormous? Or something—it could not be—to eat? What could it—

"Now," said Perub, "keep your eyes closed and cup your hands carefully. There," he said gently and laid a warm and furry body in Irun's palms. "Open your eyes."

Irun caught her breath, looking down at the little cat nestled in her hands. It was not, like most cats of the country, honey-orange with faint stripings. It was an entirely special cat of silver-grey, with eyes and ears outlined in black, as if with kohl. The eyes, staring up at her, were green as—green as—

"Her eyes," said Perub, "reminded us of the lakes in the Oasis. Green like them. We called her Ta-she, *land of lakes*. Though of course you may name her what you wish."

The little cat, not quite a kitten but almost, purred confidently in Irun's hands. "Ta-she," said Irun. "Ta-she." She looked up at her father, her own eyes brimming. "Oh, Father, how lovely—how wonderful of you—how beautiful, beautiful she is."

"Yes," said Perub. "She is beautiful. She was given me by one of the nomads of the desert. I gave him a jewel for one of his wives, in return for this jewel for you."

· "How can I thank you?"

"I have been thanked. I am looking at the face of a happy person, and that is excellent thanks."

"Why didn't you bring her with you? I could have had her an extra whole night and nearly a day."

Perub shook his head and sighed. "See, already intimations of loss begin to blur your pleasure."

"Oh, no—"

"Oh, yes. I sometimes think the gods were having a cruel game, when they gave us our minds that can look backward and forward. Better be Ta-she and live now, this moment, in your loving hands, in the sun, with no recollection of the trip just finished and no apprehension of what lies ahead. Well, enough of that. And we chose to have her come on the kitchen boat, my daughter, because we didn't wish to confine her to a cage. On my boat the chances of her falling overboard were too great. There is barely room on it for your mother and me and the captain and the rowers. She'd have got tangled in our feet, or been swept into the river by an oar. So, in the interests of her safety, you were denied a night and most of a day of her company. You think we were wrong?"

"Oh, no," Irun breathed. "Of course not."

"Well then, I suggest you hurry after Ayu and take a ride on one of the donkeys back to the house. I may be some time here with Kafa and Menferi."

Irun smiled and slipped away. Glancing back, she saw that her father was too busy to note whether she ran or walked, took a donkey or just trudged back over the dusty road to home. She and her cat. Irun and Ta-she.

They walked.

By the time she arrived, the lodge-keeper had swung back the great wooden gates and the donkeys were proceeding into the courtyard, being herded by Ayu and his assistant around to the stable area. Irun followed them in, then went through the inner gate and around to the courtyard, where Bel was taking her ease in the pool.

She lay naked upon the water, hair swirling like dark weeds, while El-oy supported her shoulders and Ani held up her knees. She was talking busily to Fl'ret, who stood at the side of the pool and listened attentively. As she talked, Bel flicked drops of water into the face of Ta-ka-lo, who lay at the pool's edge, watching her.

Bel glanced across the pool. "Ah, you've been with your father all this time? You've been given your kitten, I see. Do you like her?"

"Yes."

"You should have seen the tent of the nomad from whom we bartered her. That cat represents a remarkably fine amethyst. But the nomad's tent! All silk and tassels and cushions like clouds. Glorious. What are you going to name your kitten?"

"Ta-she."

"The name your father chose. It suits her. You may keep her in your room with you."

Irun, who'd fully intended to keep the kitten with her, nodded and said thank you. She turned away, turned back. "I do not want—do not think that she should have her claws removed."

"Well, of course not." Bel put up a wet tapering hand to fondle Ta-ka-lo's head. "She's only a little cat. Not a great savage like my beauty here."

Irun walked away, hearing Bel's light laugh following. "You must bring out qualities in her, Fl'ret, that I certainly cannot. Or see them where I don't."

Fl'ret did not reply. Not that Irun heard.

In her room, she sat on the floor and released the little cat, who flattened to her belly and began to prowl, sniffing out the scope and nature of this new environment.

"Poor little lovely," Irun crooned. "What a *time* you've had. Swept from your home in the desert, carted along on a donkey's back, sailed for miles and miles and days and days on a great barge on a brown river that surely is nothing like the clear green lakes of your oasis. Now, tell me, Ta-she, are you going to grieve and pine for what you've lost, or are you going to settle down with me and be absolutely adored? What do you say?"

The grey cat turned her striking head with its kohl-lined eyes and ears and studied Irun's face a moment. Then she leaped, twisted in mid-air, landed lightly, ran around the room, over the bed, under the bed, leaped upon a pile of cushions and crouched there, green eyes gleaming, tip of tail twitching.

"I'd think you were laughing," Irun said, "when you look at me that way. Here—" She put out her hand. As her fingers touched Ta-she, sparks flew from the grey fur. "Proving," said Irun, "that you are divinely descended. Only cats and the gods can make the air sparkle around them. But look—you must be tired. Let me tickle your ears. Go to sleep."

Ta-she, under the spell of having the back of her ears so expertly rubbed, purred and sighed and dropped abruptly off to sleep. Irun smiled down at her.

"*You certainly are no Posey*," she said. Hearing herself, she added, almost in the same tone she'd been using to the cat, "Demon, if you *want* to stay with me, and it would seem that you do, will you please not persist in using this strange tongue and saying these things that nobody but you can understand? That is *not* asking too much in return for a human body to dwell in, is it? I warn you, if you don't behave that doctor will drive you out with his horrible abominable spells and medicines and then where will you be? I'll be dead, of course, because the next time he treats me he'll kill me, and that'll leave *you* out in the cold. See?"

Fl'ret, coming through the curtain of beads, threw her hands above her head. "O Great Isis, what are you doing now, Irun? Talking to yourself as if there were another person in the room! I am driven mad with the burden of secrecy you have impo—"

"I was talking to Ta-she," Irun said calmly, stroking the sleeping cat's back.

"Is that true?" Fl'ret asked, her strained expression relaxing somewhat. "It *was* the cat?"

"It was the cat. So make yourself easy, dear Fl'ret."

"Easy!"

"Look, isn't she beautiful, my little Ta-she. And wholly her own self. Not like that poor beast Ta-ka-lo."

Fl'ret shook her head. She, too, felt sorry for Ta-ka-lo and at the same time found him repellent.

"Did she have a lovely gossip with the Governor's wife?"

"Your lady mother and the wife of the Governor found much to say to each other."

"I imagine so. I hope Bref-ni will be happy with her merchant in all his plumage. We saw a Syrian vessel go by while we were waiting for the barge. I never saw so much hair. On their heads and their faces and their *chests*, even. But, you know, Fl'ret—they seemed so cheery. They were singing away, even the men at the oars. Really singing, you know. Not chanting to keep rhythm. And they waved to other ships as they passed and called out hails. Maybe Bref-ni will be happy."

"I very much doubt that a young woman from our land can go to a lonely country far away and—"

"Why should it be lonely?"

"There will be none of her people there."

"There'll be her husband's people."

"Strangers. Barbarians. There will be nothing for her to do but pine and die. Piankhy, of course, will never accept her back."

"But why shouldn't she thrive and be happy instead? Maybe she'll *like* it in another land."

"Come, I'll have no more of it. If you are constrained by your illness to think these things, then for the sake of the promise I so rashly made you, please keep such extravagance from your speech. We of the land of Nilus are The People—all else are savages, good enough to trade with. Or war with, if it is unavoidable. But *not* to marry and live with. And I'll hear no more."

"Oh, all right," Irun said pacifically. "It's just that I don't—"

"Enough!"

"*Okay.* I mean, all right, Fl'ret. I submit to your wishes. Isn't my Ta-she gorgeous. See how she sleeps!"

"She sleeps like a cat." But Fl'ret smiled. "Yes, she is a lovely looking animal, most odd and unusual. I would advise you at the party not to let the young Pharoah see her. He is a very acquisitive boy, and likes odd things, and takes what he likes."

"He wouldn't take my cat from me!"

"He would take anything he wished from you, including your life. He's not apt to want that. But a cat of this unusual appearance—"

Irun jumped to her feet. "How could he *dare*!"

"Little Mistress, you are causing me the *greatest* distress. How can you, a child, a girl, question the will of the Pharoah?"

"He's a child himself, scarcely older than I am."

"He is the God-King, Pharoah, son of Amon, and his will is supreme, and if you do not remember that, then this demon within waxes stronger by the hour and by the time my promise of silence is up you may be so entirely in its power that the doctor will find *no* potion or incantation to drive it out, and *I* shall be blamed. Perub will throw me to the Nile crocodile."

"Oh, Fl'ret. How foolish. My father would never hurt anybody. You know that."

"Then your mother would have me thrown into the river for neglecting you in her absence."

"I think she might give you a gold amulet."

At that Fl'ret's face clouded with an expression so anxious that Irun said hastily, "I was jesting. Fl'ret. Just making a jest. Why is the King coming to the party?" she went on. "And if he does why should he see my cat? Ta-she will stay here in the women's quarters, and you shall have the pleasure of guarding her."

"He is coming because he has been invited and was gracious to accept, which has made your lady mother very happy, as you can imagine. The young King does not honor every household in this fashion. He has just made your father one of The Unique Friends of the King and to signify the honor is coming to the feast."

"My father says that he's made so many people Unique Friends that uniqueness begins to lie only in not being one."

Fl'ret beat her brow with the back of her hand. "You come by your headstrong ways and mad notions rightfully. How could he say such a thing, and how dare you repeat it?"

"I only repeated it to you, dear Fl'ret. And you would never repeat."

"No more should you. To *anyone*."

"I shall be a very sphinx in future. And then won't you be sorry."

Fl'ret sniffed. "I shall be content to stay here guarding your cat, providing your lady mother does not require me to help at the party."

"She says that I can be at the party. Does that mean I may if I wish, or I must?"

"Must, I should think. Anyway, why would you not wish to? It will be a magnificent affair. Your mother is busy planning every detail."

"I noticed how busy she was."

"She was giving me instructions for Remunum, and for the cooks and serving maids, as she relaxed in the pool. The King is bringing his musicians and his troupe of acrobats and dancers, and your father has brought dates and figs of great size and perfection from the Oasis, and Ayu is to play his harp. And now

I must go to Kafa and Remunum and discuss with them what the cooks are to prepare."

"What will it be?"

"Oh, a fine feast—spitted beef and pig, roast pigeons and ducks and reed birds, bread in shapes, all manner of fruit and vegetables, sweetmeats with honey, date wine and pomegranate wine and grape wine and beer of our own brewing. We shall have scented candles, and extra fine garlands for the guests—" Fl'ret sighed. "I should like to go to the party, but if Little Miss requires me to dance attendance on her cat—"

"Oh, Fl'ret, don't tease. I know. We can put my inlaid chest across the doorway and pile cushions all around it. It is large and heavy and the cushions would make a great bulk. I do not think such a small cat could escape a barrier like that, do you?"

"I should think not. I must go to the stewards. I'll be back presently. Why don't you go and visit with your lady mother?"

"I think I'll stay here and string beads and wait for Ta-she to waken."

Fl'ret shrugged slightly and left. Irun settled down with a box of faïence and glass beads and began to string them on a wire.

But in a few moments she put these things aside and leaned her head on her arms and cried quietly, hoping Fl'ret would not return until she had done. She needed to cry and needed time to finish crying, without interruptions or displays of concern on anyone's part. Ta-she, who wakened and stole onto her lap and then to her shoulder, to lick a couple of tears from her cheek, was not an interruption.

"Listen,' she said, sniffling, "listen to me, Ta-she. On the night of the party you must stay here in this room every moment, do you understand? You must not come out to where the party is, in the courtyard and reception rooms, because that abominable little Pharaoh might covet you and—"

She caught her breath in terror.

CHAPTER SEVENTEEN

No citizen of this land, no minion of Pharaoh's—which all of them in this land were—ever ventured to question in any way the perfection, the godliness of the King. Not even in the mind could Pharaoh be doubted, in any particular, in any fashion.

Irun recalled how once, quite long ago, she had gone with her father to the King's palace, her father having to report on the condition of the wine harvest in the Lesser Oasis. He had swung her to his shoulders and mounted his light chariot and driven off before Bel could protest that a child had no place in such an august enterprise as an audience with the King.

It must have been, indeed, a very long time ago, for her to have nestled so easily on Perub's broad shoulders, and yet she could remember the ride, swinging and bouncing over the rutted road, the span of horses cantering, sending fowl and beast and human scurrying out of their path, the cool north breeze in her face,

and Perub shouting with amusement as she clutche
his forehead with her hands and dug her heels into h
armpits.

They had arrived at the palace breathless an
laughing and covered with dust.

"Here," Perub had said, leaping from the chari
and handing the reins to the porter. "Have someor
walk them a while and then water them. There's
good fellow," he added. Perub was known for an od
distaste he had for issuing orders and a habit of add
ing a friendly word or gesture to make an order seer
a request. Bel sometimes taxed him for this, but gen
ly, since Bel could never be sharp with her husbanc
A woman in public was naturally subservient to he
lord but in private could be as much of a scold as
was in her to be. Piankhy's wife, the mother of Faye
and Semary, of Bref-ni and Sen'ti and young Ay-hel
the baby son, was known far and wide as a virag
and yet no one had ever heard her say a word tha
was not meek and truckling. No one outside her fam
ily, that is. Fayet and Semary, whose tongues wer
loosely hinged, told the things that their mother saic
and no amount of punishment ever stopped them. Th
day after the Vizier and his wife had had a battle, th
details were all over the nome and smirking face
were averted as Piankhy strode angrily about his af
fairs.

Bel, however, was if anything kinder and softer in
private than she was in public. It was only when Irur
was too much in evidence that she tended to ge
sharp-tempered, high-strung. "She'll devour you, i
you don't watch out," Bel would warn Perub, and Irur
would think to herself that there'd be nothing left t
devour by the time *she* had done with him.

But now and then, not often, Perub would scoop up his daughter and carry her off with him, as he had this morning when they'd gone to the landing stage together. As he had that day long ago when he'd gone to report to the King.

Irun could remember the breathtaking size and splendor of the palace. It made her father's mansion, and even the Vizier's palace, seem only slightly grander than a farmer's hut. Here the outer wall was so high and long that it might have enclosed a temple. Within, there were so many buildings that Irun could not recall now what most of them had looked like or what their purpose had been, except that they were all exceedingly grand. She saw in her mind only the vast inner courtyard and a lake beyond where three papyrus boats were moored, and beyond that the most glorious garden that Irun could imagine. She remembered flycatchers skimming over the orchard where bitter apple trees were in blossom. She remembered the sad, flutelike call of the shrike.

Perub had been conducted to one of the smaller reception rooms, larger than the largest room at home, where the old Pharaoh—who had since died, leaving the throne to his grandson, the present young Pharaoh—was pacing around and around, his shoulder touching the wall. He staggered from time to time and was instantly assisted by two great bodyguards, who propped him against the wall again and kept pace with his pacing. Around and around the vastness of the "small" reception room they went, Pharaoh and his bodyguards. All furniture had been moved to the center so that the King's progress around the four walls should not be impeded.

It seemed to Irun, remembering the scene, that

there had been a blurred line on the murals, just at shoulder height to the King, all around the room. But perhaps she had imagined that. What she remembered certainly was that the King had been quite drunk. Spittle had run down the sides of his mouth, and from time to time he had let out a roar of anguish and put out a still mighty arm in a blind, imperious gesture, whereupon one of the bodyguards would thrust a golden goblet of wine into the clutching hand and the royal progress would halt for a moment while the King gulped, draining the goblet and flinging it from him. The mosaic floor was littered with golden cups and sticky with spilt wine.

Irun remembered, too, that her father had actually half turned to leave—hoping, she supposed, to get her out of the besotted regal presence. But he'd checked himself immediately. One did not leave the presence of the King, even a King who was for all reasonable purposes unconscious of one's presence, until given leave.

So Perub had taken a deep breath, delivered a short description of the grape harvest of the Lesser Oasis, predicting a record wine year as to quantity and quality. He had waited then until the King had flapped his arms in what might be taken for a gesture of dismissal. Bowing deeply and backing all the way, he'd made for the door, Irun still on his shoulders. The King had not, apparently, taken heed of his presence or observed his leave-taking. Irun would always remember sitting on her father's shoulders, watching the wild old man lunging down the room, screaming with pain.

Later, her father had told her that the old Pharaoh

suffered from his teeth. That all the teeth in his head were angry and rotten and that the pain was of such measure that only wine could still it, and that not very well. Wine, it seemed, had killed in the end not only the pain but the King. No one, anywhere, ever said that, or implied it in a tone or a glance. It was a substratum knowledge forever buried, because the King was the King and without flaw.

The next God-King, the next Pharaoh, had succeeded to the throne at the age of five. His mother was his regent, but not a regent such as Hatshepsut had been. This queen had so little mind of her own that she'd begun listening to the advice of Pharaoh when he had little more than eight years on this earth, driving the Vizier and the Royal Chamberlain and the ministers half mad. Subtly, obsequiously, but firmly, Piankhy had moved in to take the reins and had held them until recently, when the Pharaoh had married his sister, Mery-ti. Mery-ti and her husband were a headstrong pair, aware of their sovereignty and determined to exercise it, which had left the Vizier with little choice but to hand it over.

Publicly or privately, no one questioned the behavior of the King.

But here am I, Irun thought frenziedly, crying with a cat and calling the King an abomination, and where does all this *take* me?

"Somewhere, Ta-she," she said, "somewhere there is another place, another time—*Gandy!*" she said suddenly. "*Gandy, gandy, gandy*—what does *gandy* mean?"

She started as Fl'ret put a hand on her arm. "Irun, my little lotus," she whispered, "you are driving me into a fever with your sounds and your strangeness. How can I keep a promise that I shall not be released from for two days and three nights?"

"You must keep it," Irun whispered back. "Why are we whispering?"

"Because speaking aloud makes the matter more real—if anything about this can be said to be real." But Fl'ret's voice returned to normal, as if she despondently accepted the fact that whispering was going to be of no help to them.

"There's no help for us," she said, shaking her head from side to side.

Irun, all at once lighthearted, jumped up and kissed Fl'ret's nose. "Don't be silly," she said. "Darling Fl'ret, we shall live together happily, the four of us, and grow to a vast old age and then go West together."

"Four of us?" Fl'ret said gloomily.

"You and me and Ta-she and the demon. *Her* name is *Erin.*"

"Erin."

"*Okay, Flora?*"

"*Okay, Erin,*" said Fl'ret, and the two of them stared at each other in wild wonderment.

CHAPTER EIGHTEEN

In the courtyard around the pool and in the gardens beyond, torches were lit and burning steadily, dipping just a trifle in a mild breeze from the north. In lofty reception rooms, lamps of rose alabaster and schist glowed tenderly, linen wicks burning in the ben oil of the moringa tree. Perfumed candles lent a soft and aromatic atmosphere. The columns in the main hall were painted dark red, ending in papyrus capitals. Between them were bright frescoes of trees with birds and insects crowding the branches, serpents entwining the trunks, and fish swimming in a painted river that went around the lowest part of the wall. The ceiling was painted to represent the sky by night at one end and by day at the other, so that the impression was one of being in a strange out-of-doors. In the great room beyond, tables were already set up around the walls, with roast meats cut to finger size, huge bowls of fruits and vegetables, leeks and melons, pomegranates and lettuces, dates and figs, bread in shapes, and all manner of honeyed cakes. On the roof, too, which overlooked the pool and courtyard and garden, low tables were set out with lamps burning and games laid out upon them. Everywhere were flowers in exquisite vases.

Irun, wearing her faïence collar, gold anklets, and a little skirt, wandered among the serving girls, who wore even less than she did. They were putting the last touches to the rooms, arranging rush mats and cushions on the floor. Ayu and Kafa were setting up two gold-inlaid chairs for the King and Mery-ti. They had been made especially for this occasion by the finest cabinetmakers and artists in the nome. There were chairs also for the Vizier, the Governor, the Royal Chamberlain, and their wives, and for very elderly guests. Perub and Bel had had their own chairs brought from their quarters.

"Oh, it all looks so pretty," Irun said to El-oy. "How nice it would be if there weren't any guests coming. We could look at all this and smell it and touch it and eat some of it and give what we couldn't eat to people who never get figs or pomegrantes or roasted beef or goose. We could share it all and not have to have the house crowded all night with people."

El-oy smiled but did not reply. Both she and Irun knew that the party would indeed last until Re indicated his divine presence in the east, and that after the King and his wife had made their ceremonial appearance and departed again, a kind of frenzy of elation would seize the guests in their joy at having been in the presence of the God-King and their infinite relief at no longer being in it. Laughter and shouting and dancing and drunkenness would ensue—and in the light of tomorrow morning this beautiful scene would look like the conclusion of a massacre.

Fl'ret had fastened the long curl over Irun's left cheek with the gold butterfly pin. She'd applied a little green malachite to her lids and outlined her eyes with kohl. "There!" she'd said, sounding pleased. "Look at yourself, Irun."

Irun had looked in the silver mirror. "Why, *look* at me, Fl'ret. I look like Ta-she."

"You do, you do. A little cat, after all. Not a small ibis."

"Miaow."

They'd laughed, and set about blocking the entrance to their room with the large chest and a mountain of cushions. Standing on tiptoe on the other side, Irun had warned Ta-she to stay and not wander until the party was over. "At least," she whispered piercingly, "until the King and Mery-ti have gone. You hear me?" She had left food and water in the room, and now could only pray that the little cat would, should she be awakened by the sound of music and laughter and clapping of hands, find the barrier impenetrable. She hadn't much hope, in truth, of the last, cats being the lithe and resourceful creatures they were. Well, then, she'd keep an eye out for her pet, and perhaps by the time Ta-she did work her way out to the reception rooms, if she did, no one would notice if Irun just grabbed her and disappeared.

Impossible. Bel would notice if she disappeared. Having asked Irun to the party, she would expect her to remain, as she would expect the lesser guests to last the party out. The King and his nobles could make their own time of arrival and departure, but most of those invited would be relied upon to remain until Bel signaled the end of the festivities. Well, it would be a long night.

Irun stood awhile, gazing at the great pyramid of fruit. She thought about the pyramids at Gizeh, and wondered if one day she would see them. Seti said that when, long ago, the pyramids had been constructed, they'd been covered with gleaming white limestone and capped with cones of pure gold. Robbers had, some centuries past, made off with the gold cones—no one knew how. And the limestone casing was gradually being hacked away for other construction. But Seti said the pyramids were awesome still in their size and splendor. He said the Sphinx at Gizeh was hundreds of times the size of any in the Avenue of Sphinxes here at the Great Temple. He said its presence was so vast and calm that just gazing at it made the spirit reposeful.

Well, maybe one day—

Ani appeared at the door and beckoned to her with a crooked finger. "Your lady mother wishes to see you, Little Miss."

Inspect me, Irun thought, following Ani to her mother's room.

"There you are," said Bel. "Come in and let me see you. Closer, Irun. Don't just stand there by the door."

Irun crossed the room reluctantly. Her mother was sitting on a small three-legged stool, having her legs and feet rubbed with fragrant oil by one of her handmaidens. Ta-ka-lo lay beside her, fur glowing like coals in a brazier, moody, joyless eyes staring at the floor. Across the bed lay a robe of gauffered pleated linen, fine as air and lightly starched, dyed a pale rose. Most of the women would be wearing white, and

Bel would move among them like a soft-hued flamingo. The jewelry she planned to wear was piled on a small table beside her, and Ani now returned to adorning a high-piled wig with a gold gem-studded chain.

"Oh, how I wish I didn't have to wear that thing," Bel said irritably, glancing at the wig. Her own hair fell nearly to her shoulders, but even its luxuriance was not sufficient for such an evening. Most women wore their hair cropped short or even shaved their heads and relied wholly on wigs. But Perub liked his Bel to have real hair he could caress or tug at playfully.

"It's a beautiful wig, Madam," said Ani.

"Oh, I know. But it's too bad that only the queen can cover her hair entirely with a—" Bel broke off, glanced with insolent nervousness at her servants and her daughter, then shrugged and laughed.

How she'd love to wear a crown, Irun thought. And continued with dispassionate honesty—she'd look marvelous in one. The young queen, Mery-ti, wore a shorter version of the tubular blue crown-hat that Nefertiti had made famous. Mery-ti looked lovely in it, but Bel would have been as beautiful as Nefertiti herself. Well, it must be frustrating for her, Irun thought indifferently.

Now Bel lowered the mirror in which she'd been studying her delicately painted face. She looked at Irun.

"Well," she said after a moment. "Well, I'm—very pleased. Fl'ret did beautifully with you. Turn around."

Irun revolved.

"Yes. Very nice. Don't you think so, Ani?"

"Yes, Madam."

"Well, then. Run along, Irun. Have fun tonight."

Yes, Madam. Irun ran along.

Her father was walking on the far side of the pool and she went around to him. He was heavily wigged, dressed in a long robe caught at the waist with a belt of gold links. He wore gold bracelets on his muscular forearms and gilded leather sandals. His toenails were dyed with henna.

"You're so *beautiful*," Irun said, reaching on her toes to give him a quick kiss.

"Am I, now? Well, let me tell you, *you* are ravishing."

Irun ducked her head. "Fl'ret says I look like Ta-she."

"You know, you do, rather. Like a little cat. And now, are you looking forward to tonight's festivities?"

"Are *you*?"

"Oh—I don't mind a party now and then. Of course, your mother just revels in them. As she should, as she should. She gives a magnificent party. Tonight, with the King and his wife coming—that's quite a triumph for your mother."

"But *you* are The Unique Friend of the King," Irun said slyly.

Perub's lips quirked. "No impertinence, Miss. How *is* Ta-she, by the by?"

"She's asleep now. I hope. Fl'ret said that if the king sees her he might even want her, *so* unusual and elegant is she. And so *very* covetous is he. So I blocked the doorway to my room and ordered her to stay there. Ordering *cats*, of course—" She shook her head. "I'll just have to hope. And keep an eye out for her. Doesn't it all look *gorgeous*?" she said, sweeping her arms wide.

They stood together, surveying the scene, the real one, and the reflection in the pool, where the light of the torches quivered and carp moved in flickers of gold. Blossoming acacia mingled its fragrance with that of the perfumed candles. In the garden, cicadas kept up an incessant humming, a harsh and agreeable music. The whiteness of moonlight lay over all.

Everywhere servants waited in readiness for the guests to arrive. The porter at the gate, his staff of office in his hand. Handmaidens with wreaths of lotus flowers that they'd woven that day and would drape around each arrival's shoulders. Men and women servants who would show the guests in and guide them to the receiving line. As if, thought Irun, this was Pharaoh's palace and they couldn't *see* the reception room, right there across the pool. Well, *she* liked things done in style, and somehow nothing she did ever seemed ridiculous, even when it was ridiculous.

"Uh-oh," said Perub. "Here's Rahmose, the Governor, and his family, What are they doing, arriving so early? Your mother will be furious."

"His Excellency, the governor of the Nome, Rahmose, and his lady-wife, Tyi, and his son, Seti!" boomed the voice of Remunum, steward of the household. The words carried across the pool, over the wall, as far, Irun was sure, as the tombs across the river on the west bank. Maybe to the next world. Remunum had a tremendous voice in which he took great pride.

Tonight the effect of his announcement was to send Ani and Fl'ret flying to the scene to be sure he hadn't lost his mind. The two of them gaped at the advancing Governor and his wife—she looking perturbed and discomposed—and sped back toward the private apartments of Perub and Bel, where they would, Irun realized, even now be assuring an unprepared mistress that she'd do well to be prepared immediately.

Perub clicked his tongue with irritation and started around the pool with a broad smile. "Rahmose, my friend! And Tyi! You are looking magnificent, my dear Tyi. And here is Seti, no longer a sapling but nearly a tree!"

"Dispense with all that, Perub," Rahmose said, jerking his hand through the air as though swatting bugs. "I realize we are unpardonably early and wish you would send someone with my profound apologies to your lady-wife. I *had* to come to see you on a matter of business—appalling matter—and since Tyi and Seti were ready—well, they just came along. I mean, I brought them along. Tyi didn't—well, no matter. Very wrong of us, no doubt. Should have had them come later—"

The usually calm Rahmose was almost babbling and kept rubbing his jaw with the back of his hand.

"Not at all, not at all," said Perub. "Any time you come, you do us honor."

One of the serving maids was attempting to put a flower garland around Rahmose's neck, after which she would adorn his wife and then even Seti if she felt he looked old enough. But until Rahmose would accept the offering she could not proceed, and he was too busy trying to grasp Perub's arm and lead him away to notice.

His wife began to speak, lifted her shoulders a little, and fell silent. Seti looked on with apparent amusement and Irun watched Seti, glad that he was here so she'd have someone to talk to. Even at a party in her father's house, she had a nervous need to be sure of someone's attention. She could always rely on Seti to be, not just polite, but truly friendly.

"Rahmose," Perub was saying. "Please accept this lotus garland as a token of our affection. If you do not accept it, you will hold us all up here just inside the gate for the rest of the evening."

"What? Oh—oh, for the love of Bes! All right, girl, give it to me." He bent slightly, so that the small serving girl could toss the wreath around his shoulders, but straightened before she'd finished. The garland ripped, spilling flowers and leaves at their feet.

"Another, please," Perub said gently, smiling at the girl. "Rahmose, will you please allow this garland, token of our affection, to be draped about your shoulders? Then we can get on with what's troubling you."

"Troubling me! *Troubling* me! Wait until you hear, and you'll see who's troubled besides me." But he stooped and waited until the garland was well around his neck before straightening again.

"Well then, tell me," said Perub.

"Let us walk." Rahmose dragged Perub in the direction of the pool, speaking in tones so loud with rage and astonishment that his words carried clearly to all present.

"The workers at the necropolis are not working!"

"Not working?"

"That's what I said. *Not working*. They have all— well, not all, but the sculptors and the artists—have sat down against the wall and have said they will not work. Actually informed me, through my steward, that they *will not work!*" Rahmose's tone was feverish. "They just sit there and refuse to budge, and according to my steward, the carpenters and masons are eying them with interest. What if they *all* refuse to

187

work? What then? What of our tombs that we're building, what of the tombs of our ancestors that must be kept in repair? What do you *say* to all this, Perub?"

"I'm so astounded I can scarcely say anything."

"Well you might. Not say anything," Rahmose sputtered. "Well you might not, indeed! Ever since I heard, I have been *dumbstruck!*"

Irun, looking at Seti, thought he grinned faintly.

"Why are they refusing to work?" Perub asked.

"They say they have not been paid for eighteen days. They say they have not had their wages of vegetables and fruit, of fat and oil and clothing. They say that *if* they are not paid they will not go back to work!" The Governor's voice rose to a crescendo of anger and bewilderment.

"What have you done about it? Have you done anything yet?"

"I've ordered the overseers to beat them with whips!"

Perub frowned. "That does not seem the way to treat artists."

"Artists! Traitors, cankerworms, evil-doers, destroyers—"

"Have they destroyed anything?" Perub asked sharply.

"Not actually with their hands destroyed anything. Yet. But think of what this action is bound to wreak in the way of destruction! Think if such a notion spreads! Think of our ancestors, think of the gods, think of ourselves! Three of those artists are painting my coffin—*were* painting my coffin—and one of the sculptors is supposedly working on my sarcophagus—and if this continues I am going to need them both at any moment, and now—" He threw his hands out, catching the blue lotus garland, once again scattering petals and leaves around him. "I tell you, Perub, if the King hears of this—why the hand of Pharaoh will erase them from existence. *Erase them*, I say!"

"Well, we won't find other artists so good very readily. Those are the best in the land. There are some likely apprentices in the necropolis, but would you want one of them to begin his profession seriously on *your* sarcophagus?"

"Ahhh!" Rahmose bellowed like a water buffalo.

Seti put a hand across his mouth, and Irun felt a laugh gather inside her.

"Children," said Tyi. "Perhaps you could go up on the roof and play at Hounds and Jackals. Or something. Anyway, you had better go."

"Come on, Seti," said Irun. They ran up the brick stairs to the flat roof above the great reception rooms and gallery where, lying on the floor at the edge of the loggia, they could rest their chins on their hands and get an even better view of the consultation between Rahmose and Perub.

Other guests were arriving, being announced by Remunum. But all was confusion. Irun could just picture her mother, waiting for Perub to join her so the reception line could commence, while Perub and Rahmose, and now the Vizier himself, accompanied by the Royal Chamberlain, wrangled at the edge of the pool over what to do about insurrection in the necropolis.

She'll be furious, Irun thought. She will be incarnadine with ire. How dared they—those madmen across the Nile, those workers, peasants, *offal*—how dared they do such a thing, and if they *had* to contrive such a death-deserving action, *how dared they do it on the day of her party?*

Irun hugged herself with pleasure. Ignoble of her. Unseemly. Nonetheless, delicious. Aside from the catastrophe of *me*, of my existence, my continual presence as her daughter, her sole and wholly unsatisfactory child, aside from *that*, she's never been thwarted before in her life, probably. And there she is—if Irun had hung by her feet from the balcony and *looked*, she could not have been surer of Bel's appearance—there she is, maybe the most beautiful woman along the whole length of the Nile, at her place in the receiving line with no husband beside her and her party milling around like a bunch of sheep in a pen who have just heard the distant roar of the lion.

"Isn't it funny?" she said to Seti.

"I'm not sure. But it *seems* funny. They're bawling and cackling like a lot of animals."

"Just what I was thinking. Look, Sen'ti is going to herd Fayet and Semary up here with us. Probably they think they're getting us out of the way, so we won't hear."

Fayet and Semary appeared on the roof and ran across to where Seti and Irun were lying. For once Irun didn't even trouble to look at them and compare herself unfavorably. She just motioned to them to lie down and be quiet.

"I'll send the guard over! I'll send the soldiers!" Piankhy was saying. "If the overseers can't whip them into submission then we'll kill them. As an example to the others."

"But four of those artists have been working on my coffin and sarcophagus, and in the interior of my tomb for years!" Rahmose protested. "I will not have them killed before they're finished!"

"That would have to go for the others, too," Piankhy

said, his great brow furrowed like an irrigation ditch beneath his wig. "I've had a sculptor, Yunet, the best of them all, working on a statue of me for I don't know *how* long."

"Fl'ret," Perub called out. Fl'ret, run into my quarters and bring me that piece of limestone I brought back from my visit to our tomb the other day. Wait, wait," he exhorted the men around him. "I want to show you something. Ah, here you are, my dear." He put an arm around Bel, who had stormed up to him. "I regret this deeply," Perub said. "Your party—"

"My party is a shambles, that's what it is!" Bel's voice was shaking, very nearly shrill. "Please come back and stand with me. If we go into the reception room and stand there, people will be obliged to form a line and be received and maybe we can— Oh, Fl'ret, what are you *doing* here? Don't *bother* me—"

"I asked her to fetch something for me, my dear. Now, be patient. Let me show this drawing to our friends here, and propose a compromise with the workers."

"Compromise! I'd compromise them into graves of fire ants, that's what I'd do. I'd compromise them into the crocodile's jaw. And that's what the King will do when he hears—"

"Oh, my dear Madam, lovely lady," said Piankhy hurriedly. "We must try in every way to avoid having the King hear of this. We must try to settle it before word reaches his ear. Fortunately, he rarely listens to anybody, so we may be able to settle the thing and still keep it from him."

"Why shouldn't he hear about it?" Bel demanded. "*He'd* know how to deal with them." She cast a scornful look about, but when she came to Perub, her glance faltered.

"The King will blame us, my dear," said Perub. "Don't you see? He will find us negligent in having permitted such a situation to arise."

"How could you know such a thing could happen? How could anyone even *dream* of such derangement?"

"That is our view," said Piankhy glumly. "It is not likely, Madam, to be the King's. We are supposed to keep order. To anticipate disorder and head it off. How anyone could have forseen *this*, of course— Well, well, Perub. You say you have an idea?"

"I want you to look at this drawing I picked up the other day at the necropolis." He handed a small stone chip to the Vizier.

"What's that?" Fayet whispered.

"A drawing on a bit of limestone," Irun said. She had seen it when her father brought it back from a visit to the tomb he was having built for himself and Bel, with an extra room for Irun, should she not marry. She leaned further over the roof's edge, trying to see, until Seti pulled her back.

"They'll see you," he said. "What's the drawing of?"

"A tiny sketch of a hippopotamus coming out of the river, with some stalks of papyrus on one side and a little bird on his head. It's really a beautiful little thing, and Father—well, you'd think he'd found a great treasure—"

"Look at this," Perub say saying. "Look at the exquisite lines, the grace and beauty of the composition, and in such miniature. And mind you, this was just a sketch some artist made and tossed aside as valueless. Now, do you think the man who made that could be *whipped* into making another such? You don't beat artistry like that into men."

"It certainly is an exquisite, and enchanting piece of work," Piankhy said, fondling the bit of limestone. "Lovely," he repeated.

Perub scarcely hesitated. "Take it, by all means," he said. Irun knew the words cost him something, but no one would have known it from his tone. She realized, too, how addled the Vizier was feeling, since in the ordinary way of things he would never admire a possession of his host's aloud, knowing that whatever the object, short of the man's wife, he would be given it.

"Oh, now," he began to protest, but gave up at a gesture from Perub. "Well, well. Thank you very much, Perub. I shall treasure it. I shall take it in my Sun Boat when I go West. But, to your idea, please."

"To begin with, I have now asked both you and Rahmose three or four times whether what the workmen say is true."

"True? What do you mean, true?"

"Piankhy, have they or have they not gone without their wages of oil and fat and so forth for eighteen days?"

"I don't know."

"And you, Rahmose? Do you know if their story is true?"

But neither Rahmose nor the Royal Chamberlain knew whether, in fact, the men at the necropolis had gone without their wages for eighteen days.

"But didn't you ask your steward to ascertain this before he had the overseers start beating them?"

"Why, no," said Rahmose. "What they were—are—doing is outrageous, unacceptable, I don't care what the reason."

"I don't agree," said Perub. He took their combined glares without flinching. "I think that if they have not been paid their just wages—"

"They have a right to stop *working*?"

"I won't go so far as that," Perub said slowly. "But I do believe they should be paid. Promptly. And then they'll go back to work and the whole thing will be settled."

"Settled," said Piankhy. "You think so. What about next time?"

"If we see to it that the overseers *pay* them—and I wouldn't put it past some of those fellows to be diverting oil and fat and clothing into their own nests at the expense of the workers—if we are more vigilant in overseeing the overseers and their bahavior, the matter should not arise again," Perub concluded doubtfully.

"Just suppose," said Rahmose, putting Perub's thought into words, "that next time, having got away with this, they decide to sit down against the wall and not work because they want *more* fat and oil and so forth for their work. What then? What lies in that direction?"

"I don't know," Perub admitted. "But can we not at least send Kafa and your stewards over to the necropolis to assure the artists and sculptors that they will be paid promptly, and then attempt to keep the entire matter from the King's attention?"

"And get on with my party."

"Of course, my dear."

"After all," Bel went on. "This is a significant, a momentous evening. The King and his wife are to be with us this evening, and you all stand around gabbling as if it were any evening's entertainment. Please, send your emissaries to those swine across the river and let us form the reception line so that the feast can be concluded before the Royal Pair arrives."

The King, who would take no food except in the palace, would arrive expecting all signs of viands, however delicious, to be erased. He would have with him his wine taster and would accept, from the most beautiful goblet in Bel's possession, a sip of wine if the taster, drinking from a plain goblet, wine from the same ewer, did not show signs of poison within fifteen minutes and was still alive in thirty.

Piankhy, Rahmose, Perub, and the Royal Chamberlain summoned their stewards and consulted with them earnestly as more and more guests arrived and were announced and left to shift about restlessly, eying one another, waiting—

CHAPTER NINETEEN

After Kafa and the other stewards had departed to take one of the Vizier's boats across the Nile to the west bank where the necropolis lay, Bel at last succeeded in getting her receiving line in action. Seti and Irun, Fayet and Semary, did not go down for it, knowing that while they were welcome to be at the party, it was actually a function for grownups. They would certainly not be missed.

Instead, they retained their excellent watching post and commented on the people arriving in their finery, weaving in a snake line from the outer court, where they descended from their chariots, which were taken away by stablemen, into the courtyard, past the pool, and so into the great reception room. They could not see into the room, which was under the loggia, but could picture it. Perub and Bel would be standing, dazzling in their good looks, their fine raiment and jewelry, no trace of the recent dissension on their features. They would speak to each person passing, pressing a hand, leaning forward to lay a light kiss on the brow of a favored guest.

The whole process took over an hour. The candles and lamps made a golden glow, the moon a white sheen over the courtyards, the pool, the gardens and orchard beyond. The spiced pungency of meats and breads and wine and beer mingled with the fragrance of acacia and eucalyptus. In a little pavilion put up at a far corner of the pool, Ayu played his harp, accompanied by a young man with a flute. The sounds of caressed strings, the sweet notes of the reed, wove through the voices of guests as they laughed and ate and drank.

When the receiving line was at last dispersed, Irun said, in as near to Bel's hostess tone as she could summon, "Let us go down and eat."

They trooped down and, with other quite young people, sat on rush mats out near the pool. Serving men and girls passed great trays of roast fowl and beef cut to finger size, and bread in shapes, and fruits and cakes. The food was delicious, but Irun found she couldn't eat much, she was so busy devouring the look and the sound of the party. The garlanded guests nibbling, sipping, chatting. The music playing. The torches dipping, rising, reflecting in the pool. It was lovely, lovely—

Maybe I'm getting to *like* parties. Perhaps because tonight she felt that she looked nice, like a little cat?

The serving girls came with bowls of scented water. The young people dipped their hands, dried them on linen towels, and then, each taking a little faïence goblet of wine, went back up to the roof. Others had joined them. Edzme and his two brothers, Mek't and

Hakor. Kiko and Zecca, sons of Edzme's uncle, Perneb. Mery, their sister. A few more.

The girls got together to talk of clothes and jewels and what their future husbands would be like.

"What I would like to know," Fayet was saying, "is what my husband-to-be is doing now, right this minute. Where he is. Here on this roof?" Her glance went from Edzme to Hakor and moved on to Seti, where it lingered slightly. "Or in some other nome altogether?"

"Or some other land?" Mery said mischievously. "Maybe your husband will be a—will be a *Macedonian!*"

They all burst out laughing, including Fayet and Semary. Oh, Bref-ni would be long remembered, even if her father said she had never existed.

The boys, on another part of the roof, talked warfare and hunting.

Fayet and Semary, who lacked graciousness but at times displayed sketchy manners, asked Irun to join them. She was, after all, almost their hostess. But Irun wandered back to the roof's edge, where she sat trying to hear Ayu and the flute player over the babble of voices below. She noticed her father and Rahmose and Piankhy, now huddled in session with the Royal Chamberlain. Their faces wore expressions of relief, so it appeared that the troubles across the river had been, temporarily anyway, laid to rest. When Pharaoh finally saw fit to arrive no one would be obliged to inform him that an insurrection had taken place. Certainly nobody would wish to inform him. He was the God-King. He was also mettlesome, bad-tempered, and arrogant, quite likely to strike a man down for bringing him bad news. The old Pharaoh, before being felled by his teeth, had been very different.

Even in his drunkenness, Perub had said, the old King retained a penetrating glance, as though he would sink into another's being and know what thoughts were there, know the heart. This boy God-King never met anyone's eye. "He isn't blind," Perub had said, "but I never get the impression that he *sees*." Another of his reckless observations that she'd do well not to repeat.

Seti came over to where she sat. He was carrying the board and box of Hounds and Jackals. The board was laid out in ivory and ebony squares. The players were of feldspar—green for jackals, red for hounds.

"Want a game?"

Irun nodded happily.

"Why were you frowning?"

"Was I?"

"Fiercely."

"Well—I was thinking what a windbag the King is."

Seti's hand flew to his brow. "Irun," he whispered. "Are you crazy? You'd better curb your tongue, or you'll have yourself and your whole family in desperate trouble. Look—why don't you just keep quiet altogether and we'll play this game. Until you're yourself again."

"Myself." Irun giggled. Who's that?

Her hounds beat Seti's jackals badly, until he had only two left. As he sat, chin in hand, frowning over the problem, Irun studied the squares of the board. "*Chess*," she muttered.

"What's *chess*?" Seti asked. He reached for one of his jackals, withdrew his hand and looked at her. "You've got me beat."

"What did I say about *chess*?"

"You just said *chess*. What does it mean?"

Is Seti the person to tell? she wondered. I wouldn't alarm or frighten him the way I do Fl'ret, the way I probably would my father. I don't mean all that much to Seti. On the other hand, he does like me, and he does listen. He couldn't call the doctor, as Perub could and would. He would just listen, and sympathize, and maybe even have a suggestion. She could begin by saying, "Seti, look—I've got a demon. Her name is *Erin*, and she wanders back and forth in time as I wander through the rooms of this house."

"I'm not sure what it means," she said. "I mean, I am sure, but I'm not." He looked interested, so she went on. "Seti, did you ever hear the theory that time isn't something that goes forward all the time, with the past going backward, but that it's more like a snake with its tail in its mouth, without a beginning or an end?"

"The Divine Imhotep advanced that idea centuries ago."

"But then—that would mean everything is happening at once. Everything that has, and is, and is going to. Like the spots on a snake in different places, but still all there at once." He nodded. "Well, do you believe that?"

"I believe lots of things."

"Oh!" she said impatiently. "That's what my father always says. I want an *answer* to something once in a while."

"Then ask something that can be answered."

"Like what?"

Seti lifted his shoulders. "Lots of things can be. They aren't as interesting, of course. I like, myself, to think about—enigmas."

"Like what?" she said again.

"Oh—like the sky, for instance. Some people say the world ends at the sky. But how could that be? You could say it was like a ceiling, but there's always something above a ceiling. And what about what's above that? And above that?"

"That's the sort of thing you think about?"

"Sometimes. Irun!" he exclaimed in a low voice. "Look! Look there, quickly—over at the horizon!"

A shower of falling stars went down in a rain of brilliance beyond the graves of the western hills. It was there and gone but left an impression like something dazzling the eyelids.

"It's a sign," Irun whispered.

"Of what?"

"I don't think people know what signs say. It's just a *sign*." She thought it was a sign that something was going to happen tonight, more important even than a visit from Pharaoh. But she held her tongue.

They looked around. No one else here on the roof seemed to have noticed. Those below were too busy talking to pay attention to the heavens.

"Just for us," Seti said with satisfaction. "I don't know what it means, either, but I think it was meant just for us."

I think, Irun said to herself, that it wasn't meant for us or for anyone. It just happened. The stars flash out of the dark and disappear, but not for people to see. We're just people. And we flash into life and disappear, but not for the stars to see. They're just stars.

How strange, strange, strange. Being alive, feeling, thinking—

"Tell me something else you think about," she said.

"Food. I'm hungry again. Let's go down and get something to eat."

"I don't think we can. The servants are clearing away the tables, so everything will be in order when the King arrives. So the house will look as if it had been constructed for his visit and would be destroyed the moment he left. He wants no sign of human appetites around him, my father—that is, I've heard it said."

"He takes wine."

"A courtesy sip." Even a King had to observe the rules of hospitality.

From far away came the sound of a fanfare. Moaning was heard outside the walls of Perub's mansion. Moaning filled the air, drowned the chorus of the cicadas and the songs of night birds and the rustling of palms and the music of Ayu and the flute player. It increased till it seemed that the whole valley was one wailing clamor reaching over the river, over the silently tenanted hills of the west, to the vast untrackable desert beyond.

Pharaoh was approaching.

Irun touched Seti's arm. "Let's go down," she said softly. "I know a tree we can climb. We can see everything, and no one will trouble themselves about seeing us. Come on, Seti. Hurry."

They ran quietly down the staircase, raced away into the shadows of the garden, climbed almost to the top of a eucalyptus tree, and were lost to view in its leaves.

"Whew," Seti said. He was breathing hard, but not from the run or the climb. "You have a lot of nerve, Irun."

"I do, don't I?" she said in a voice part puzzled, part pleased. Not such a timid little outsider, after all.

The shrieks and cries outside the wall increased. Irun pictured what it was like out there. Crowds shoulder to shoulder, chest to back, massed for miles and nearly unable to move, straining for a glimpse of Pharaoh, Son of Amon, as he passed. There would be children, too. Babes in arms, infants on their parents' shoulders, older ones down in the crush, piping, squealing. Irun imagined them down there among the legs, frightened and begging to be lifted up.

He was coming.

He would be approaching slowly, borne on his handchair by six great gleaming slaves oiled from head to foot and shining with gold. He would be wearing the great double crown of Upper and Lower Egypt and enough jewelry to bend an average man double, but would hold himself fiercely, youthfully erect. As he passed, crushed together as they were, the populace would fight to bow its collective forehead to the ground and beat the dust with its fists, groaning at the exquisite anguish of having beheld the God. Some of those worshipers would never rise again, the crush of adulation having broken their bodies.

Behind the King would come Mery-ti, glittering, impassive, looking at the sky. In front and behind and to both sides would be the foot guards, the horse guards, the trumpeters, the heralds, and at the rear would come the musicians and the acrobats and dancers.

In the reception rooms, in the courtyard, a ripple of apprehension ran, a low dry whispering, like the stirring of locust wings. Ayu's hands fell from the harp strings, the flutist dropped the reed to his lap. Irun knew that every heart was thudding in its cage, and even the greatest palms were clammy. The God-King was terrifying, his visit an appalling honor.

Straining forward, she could see *her*, Bel, her mother. Standing very straight, breast rising and falling rapidly, eyes brilliant.

He had arrived.

As he was carried through the great gate in his blazing handchair the guests sank to their knees and touched their foreheads to the floor. At the center of the courtyard he lifted one finger. The slaves halted immediately, bent, and held the chair steady, as with the token assistance of two Royal Fan Bearers the King alit, stood upon the ground, and waited, head up, motionless. He fixed his gaze slightly upward, at a slant, so that no one could tell what he was thinking, if he was thinking, if he listened to any voice but his own voice in his crowned and regal head. His queen, Mery-ti, had adopted the mannerism. It gave them an air of monumental indifference.

Except for a single golden ewer of wine, a golden cup and a glass one, the tables were empty. The servants of the household, unequal to the royal presence, had retired into the shadows to squat there, awaiting a sign from Perub that would set them moving again. His majesty brought his own servants with him wherever he went.

He stood now, immobile as one of the colossi at Memnon, while Mery-ti's handchair was gently lowered and she was assisted by her maidens to the gleaming tiled floor.

At this, the company rose, standing with heads humbly bowed while Bel came forward, carrying two magnificent garlands, blue lotus for the King, white for Mery-ti. She knelt before the King, touched her forehead to his foot, then rose and draped a wreath about his shoulders, taking care not to touch his royal person with her fingers. Then she moved to Mery-ti and knelt, but did not lower her forehead, rose, and draped the blooms about those slender shoulders.

When both were wreathed, the two royal persons moved into the reception room, where they assumed their places on the near-thrones provided by Perub.

Lifting his finger again, the King signaled that he was ready to be entertained, then sat, arms crossed, holding in his hands the crook and flail, emblems of his divine office.

The royal musicians entered the pavilion across the pool with Ayu and the young flutist. Men with drums began to beat upon them softly. So softly, Irun thought, leaning over to watch through the leaves, that it was almost like feeling the sound at first, not hearing it. But as the tempo increased, the voice of the drums deepened. Then the tambourines joined in, and the acrobats sprang from the shadows and cart-wheeled around the pool. Their naked hairless bodies glistened and they moved in bewildering patterns of leaps and arcs, fluid and free as fish or birds, precise as arithmetic.

"You're going to fall out of the tree," Seti whispered, grabbing her arm.

"Oh, but aren't they splendid, Seti? Wouldn't you love to be able to do that?"

"I *can* do that," he said proudly, then smiled and added, "Not so well, I guess."

When the acrobats retired they were breathing as

easily as if they had sauntered around the pool, not traversed it at the speed of gazelles. Then the dancers came, girls in flower garlands and short gauze skirts. They, too, wove beautiful patterns for the delectation of the King. But Irun, staring at him through the leaves, thought he was not watching at all.

He reminds me of someone, she thought. Who does he put me in mind of? Someone, someone—but she could not summon a name or an individual. Only a misted-over picture of someone else . . . another young man, a boy, also slender and handsome and imperious. Someone whose appearance took the breath away and who was, like Pharaoh over there, leader of *the Pack*. That is, she corrected herself, of The People.

Someone—she could not remember.

As the dancers melted into the darkness, Ayu began to play his harp, accompanied by the high notes of the flute and the melancholy voice of a gold and silver trumpet.

The King, whose wine taster had withstood the test and remained upright, lifted the goblet for the first time to his lips and took a small sip as Ayu began to sing.

He sang many songs—of love, of the ease of death and going forth to the West, of the pride of ancestors and the glory of Egypt.

Irun was growing uncomfortable on her branch in the eucalyptus. She whispered to Seti, "Do you think we could climb down? Do you suppose anyone would notice?"

"No!" he whispered back. "Don't even think of it!"

"But—"

"No, no, no! And don't fall out, either!"

Ayu sang the "Song of the Herdsman."

The herdsman is in the water among the fish.
    He speaks with the shad,
        and greets the khat-fish.
O West! Whence is the herdsman?
    A herdsman of the West.

Irun felt a tear go down her cheek. Such a beautiful voice, that of the slave Ayu. And this song of the herdsman dying and going West as confidently as a nobleman—that was beautiful.

Suddenly she leaned forward again and had to clutch at a branch to steady herself.

"O Isis," she whispered. "O Bastet!"

"What *is* it?" Seti asked fiercely. "You're going to—"

"It's Ta-she, my cat. She's escaped from my room and wandered out, and now if the King sees her—but maybe he won't, maybe—"

For the first time since he'd arrived, the King looked at something. He watched Ta-she cross the courtyard, leap in air, twisting like one of his own acrobats. She landed lightly a little way from the reception room where the Royal Couple sat, and began to chase her tail.

The King lifted a finger. The music and the singing ceased. He said, "My Majesty sees a most unusual and lovely cat. Bring it to me."

Bel signaled to Remunum. "Bring the cat."

"No!" Irun shrieked, tumbling out of the tree and racing around the pool to stand in the reception room. "No, no, no!" she screamed. "You may not! That is my cat and you may not have her!"

The silence that followed was terrible. In all the world no one breathed and nothing moved, except Ta-she, who began to stalk a cricket.

The King's thin mouth seemed to disappear. His eyes, blank as the eyes of one of his own statues, were on the cat, and his jaw moved slightly as his teeth fixed together.

If I could think, Irun thought, too numb to know that she was thinking—if I could think, I'd think that this was like the moment when swollen Nilus rises too high and breaks the dykes and rides in a brown raging wall over the land, toppling houses, hurling chickens, oxen, pigs, and people, driving them into the mud. This is that ominous moment of waiting while the roar of the water approaches—a terror there is no way to confront, no way to avoid.

She became aware that she was thinking thoughts. Aware that all the company had wilted to the floor. That all were crouching, chests on knees, hands clenched on heads.

I'll unsay it, she thought. But it was too late. If she could have unsaid the words she would have unsaid them. She would have relinquished Ta-she to this awful boy whose displeasure could drive proud people to press their noses on the floor. But since it was too late, since now it was too late for unsaying or relinquishing—at least she would not bow down.

Her body sang with fear as she remained standing.

Then she felt her father's hand on her shoulder and leaned against him weakly. Just they two standing, facing the God-King on his specially built throne of ebony and ivory and gold.

Now what would happen?

"I'm here with you, Irun," said her father.

She stared at the King, whose royal features began to blur and grow hazy—his face shifting and altering until he became—a boy on a chair. Looking, in fact, sort of like—*like Fred Englund, king of a Pack of schoolkids*—

"*Can you hear me, Erin?*"

PART THREE

CHAPTER TWENTY

"Erin," said Peter Gandy. "Erin, can you hear me? I'm here with you."

Erin opened her eyes. "*Isis!* That was just in time. Except, of course, that it wasn't the King after all. Just old Fred, king of the Pack. No Pharaoh, Fred—"

Her glance swayed and slid about the room. Hospital room, apparently. There was Doctor—Doctor—she couldn't remember his name. "Anyway," she muttered, "not the kind that feeds live mice to people."

"A little disoriented," said the doctor.

"A little?" said Belle Gandy in a shaken voice.

"Just a trifle," the doctor said calmly. "Quite natural. Erin, do you know where you are?"

"Hospital, I guess."

"Do you remember what happened?"

"There was a party, and the King was just about to take my cat away from me. Rotten kid. Pharaoh or not, he's a rotten kid, but I don't know what's going to happen now—what he'll do to my father or me. Or *her*. Ruined her party—" Her lids drooped, and she dragged them open. She wasn't going back there yet.

"Oh, my God!" Belle said. "What are we going to do?"

"Belle, please," said Peter. "She's had a blow on her head—"

"A slight concussion, three stitches. She's going to be fine. Give her a little time. I think we'd better let her rest now." He leaned over the bed, putting his long fingers on Erin's forehead, then on her wrist. "Erin, we're going to leave you now for a while. The nurse will give you a pill to help you sleep, and Flora here is going to be with you all the time. Do you understand me?"

"I don't want to sleep again." She looked at her father and said languidly, "Think you there was, or might be, such a time as this I dream'd of?"

He took her hand in his. "I don't know what time you dreamed of, Missy."

"But you were there with me. And *she* was. And Fl'ret." She moved her gaze to Flora, standing at the foot of the bed, hands twisting and twining together. "You were there. Don't you remember?"

"I—"

"Well, we're not there now. I guess. No, we aren't there now. But if I go to sleep—" She sat up and was seized with dizziness. She put her hands to her head. A bandage, just above her left ear. She felt further, exploring—

"They had to shave part of your hair, for the stitches," Belle Gandy explained. "So I just told them to cut it all short. When you're better we'll go to Pepe and he'll give you a proper styling. It will look quite nice, I think."

214

"Sort of an Afro."

"Why, yes," said Belle, sounding pleased at this sensible remark.

"Now, Erin," said the doctor. "Lie back and don't try to get up until you're given permission. Is that understood?"

"I've been dizzy for such a long, long time," she murmured.

"Just a few hours."

"I wonder if I'm ever going to get over it. Maybe not. Maybe I'll just have to live with the demon, whatever her name is, and the dizziness, too, all the rest of my life—whatever that is, *wherever* it is."

"Now see here, Doctor," said Belle Gandy. "You've got to *do* something. She's positively raving."

"Will you come outside, please," said the doctor, looking at Peter Gandy, who took his wife's arm and urged her toward the door. "We won't be long," he said to Erin. "I'll—we'll be right outside here, okay?"

" 'Bye, Daddy."

When they'd gone, Erin said, "Fl'ret, *you* remember, don't you? How can you not remember?"

"Of course I remember."

Erin looked at her suspiciously. "You're humoring me."

"No."

"Then, what do you remember?"

"All that you do."

"And that's the best you're going to do for me?"

"It's all I can do for you. I always do all I can for you, you know that."

"But you were there with me."

"Yes."

"Where?"

"The place where we were."

Erin closed her eyes. They were—all of them—going to humor her. Except for Bel, who just straightforwardly thought she was cuckoo. For once she made more sense than any of the rest of them.

Am I cuckoo from a blow on the head? Erin wondered. What blow on the head? I remember waking up by the mastaba—

She put her hand to her mouth. The mastaba. Not that of Ha'tpet in the desert. The mastaba in the Metropolitan. She'd been running away from those awful minions of Fred's—they'd seemed so important, what they said had seemed so *important*—and she'd hit her head on that mastaba and then—

Had that somehow spun her back in time to another mastaba, another place, another life that she had lived and then lived partway through again? Had she gone back and then come back here, and was all that still going on back there in Perub's, her father's, mansion? Everybody impaled by the royal wrath of Pharaoh?

"Do you suppose time could be like a snake with a tail in its mouth?" she asked Flora. "Just going around, with no beginning and no end?"

"That's what Mr. Einstein thought, as nearly as I can make out."

Erin filled her lungs with air, let it out slowly. "Fl—Flora, how long have I been here?"

"Since four o'clock."

"Four o'clock what day?"

"Today."

"Today? *Today?* I've only been here since—what time is it now?"

"Nearly midnight."

"How did my parents get here so fast?"

216

"I called immediately and was lucky enough to get them at the hotel, and they took the first plane out. They've been here a couple of hours."

"I don't understand," Erin said tiredly. "I really don't understand anything at all. It's seemed like years—years and years. I've lived a whole *life*, practically. One way or another," she added, mostly to herself, "I think it was about to come to an end."

"The doctor says a concussion can cause distortions in the sense of time, confusion about everything, really. For a while. You only had a mild concussion, Erin. You'll be over this—this fancy, in no time."

"Well, of course," said Erin. "That's all it was."

A fancy. A dream. A concussed confusion. But how cleverly the brain worked in dreams, weaving in this time and that time, people from here, people from there—

The doctor let her go home three days later. Her father tended to handle her as if she were a box of eggs, and *she* keeps eying me, Erin thought, as if at any moment I'll crack and scramble myself. Well—

Flora made tea and they all sat in the living room, with the fire going, and for a while drank tea and ate little sandwiches and made little stabs at conversation.

Erin hardly listened.

No matter what they say, *I* know where I was, if not where I'm going. Maybe they were right, those who said we die and start all over and work our way back to—to this form in three thousand years. Maybe Pharaoh swept my whole family and everyone at the party that night into oblivion, and we all started trudging back, and here we are again and someday we'll die and start all over again and next time wind up—where? Maybe even on another planet.

She looked at her mother. Beautiful Bel. Beautiful Belle Gandy. *Mother*. Will she and I be slugging it out on Mars in another three thousand years? Are we never, at any period in time, going to get *along* together?

Peter Gandy stood up. "Come on, Erin. Your mother and I have a present for you. Up in your room."

"Both of you? I mean—"

"Both of us," Belle said tartly. "Your father found it and I agreed to let you keep it. So it's from both of us."

Erin and her father exchanged a smile. Then Erin said, "Well, that was very nice of you. Mother."

Belle's eyes widened. "Well," she said. "Well. Shall we go up?"

Ta-she sat in the middle of Erin's bed, looking around the room with interest. She hadn't changed a bit. The same size, same kohl-lined eyes and ears, same lake-green glance. She stood up at Erin's approach and purred.

Erin put a tentative hand out, then scooped up the little cat and held her close. "Where did you *find* her?" she breathed.

"Wandering the streets," said Peter. "She was crouched by the doorstep when I went out to get the paper yesterday morning and was still there when I left for the office. So I—we—opened the door and she walked right in. We figured she must be yours," he added with a laugh.

"She is. Her name is Ta-she."

218

"Isn't that pretty," said Belle. She looked around, looked at the cat. "We must get her a scratching post."

"Oh—that'd be *fine*."

"Very well, then. I must go down and help Flora. She's preparing a homecoming feast and I'm designated potboy. Potgirl. I don't know whether anyone else has noticed, Erin, but I've noticed that you haven't made any faces since you had your accident. Isn't that interesting?"

Erin considered saying, "Well, I'm three thousand years older. I should've got over it by now." But she didn't.

When Belle had gone, Peter Gandy sat in the pink velvet chair, eyes fixed fondly on Erin and her cat.

"Daddy, do you believe in reincarnation?"

He said, not surprising her, "I'm prepared to believe in anything."

"Well, I've decided that if there is such a thing, next time around I'm going to stop at being a cat."

"A cat's a marvelous creature. Maybe it'd be a good choice, if you could make it."

"But you wouldn't?"

"Oh, no. I'd press on to the human condition again."

"But why? You said once that animals had things better arranged."

"Did I? Still—I'd opt for human form. It's such a wonderful, dumb, brave thing to be a human being." He stood up. "It's good to have you home, Missy."

"It's awfully good to *be* home."

When they were alone, she said to Ta-she, "So you knew just where to find me, you clever, adorable creature. You knew just which age to come to and which doorstep. Oh, what a wonder you are."

Ta-she, after all, was the only one who would understand what she was talking about.

Or was she?

On the weekend, Erin was in her room, looking in the mirror at her new haircut and liking what she saw, when Flora called up the stairs. "Erin! Erin, your friend Seti is here to see you!"

"Oh, that's *super*. Tell him I'll be right there."

She fluffed her hair with a comb, pinched her cheeks a little, and ran to the head of the stairs. There he was, with clothes on his body and hair on his head, but otherwise Seti as she'd last seen him in the eucalyptus tree.

"Hello," he said, looking up at her. "How are you, Irun?"

TWILIGHT™
WHERE DARKNESS BEGINS...

☐	1	**DEADLY SLEEP**, D. Cowan	. . . .	91961-4-47	$2.50
☐	2	**THE POWER**, B. Haynes	. . . .	97164-0-49	2.25
☐	3	**THE INITIATION**, R. Brunn	. . . .	94047-8-23	2.50
☐	4	**FATAL ATTRACTION**, I. Howe	. . . .	92496-0-31	1.95
☐	5	**BLINK OF THE MIND**, D.B. Francis	. . . . . .	90496-X-35	2.25
☐	6	**VOICES IN THE DARK**, J. Haynes	. . . . . .	99317-2-25	2.50
☐	7	**PLAY TO LIVE**, C. Veley	. . . . : . . .	96950-6-56	1.95
☐	8	**BLOOD RED ROSES**, S. Armstrong	. . . . .	90314-9-19	1.95
☐	9	**DEMON TREE**, C. Daniel	. . . .	92097-3-18	1.95
☐	10	**THE AVENGING SPIRIT**, E. Stevenson	. . . .	90001-8-58	1.95
☐	11	**NIGHTMARE LAKE**, C. Laymon	. . . .	95945-4-15	1.95
☐	12	**THE TWISTED ROOM**, J.P. Smith	. . . . . .	98690-7-16	1.95
☐	13	**VICIOUS CIRCLE**, I. Howe	. . . .	99318-0-24	2.50
☐	14	**FOOTPRINTS OF THE DEAD**, J. Callahan	. . . .	92531-2-20	1.95
☐	15	**SPIRITS AND SPELLS**, B. Coville	. . . .	98151-4-	2.50
☐	16	**DRAWING THE DEAD**, N. Selden	. . . .	92141-4-22	1.95
☐	17	**STORM CHILD**, S. Netter	. . . .	98289-8-21	1.95
☐	18	**WATERY GRAVE**, J. Trainor	. . . .	99419-5-30	1.95
☐	19	**DANCE OF DEATH**, L. Kassem	. . . .	91659-3-10	2.25
☐	20	**FAMILY CRYPT**, J. Trainor	. . . .	92461-8-32	2.25
☐	21	**EVIL ON THE BAYOU**, R.T. Cusick	. . . . . .	92431-6-39	2.25
☐	22	**THE HAUNTED DOLLHOUSE**, S. Blake	. . . . .	93643-8-15	2.25
☐	23	**THE WARNING**, A. Byron	. . . .	99335-0-15	2.25
☐	24	**AMULET OF DOOM**, B. Coville	. . . .	90119-7-32	2.50

At your local bookstore or use this handy coupon for ordering:

 Dell DELL READERS SERVICE—DEPT. R678A
P.O. BOX 1000, PINE BROOK, N.J. 07058

Please send me the above title(s). I am enclosing $_____ (please add 75¢ per copy to cover postage and handling). Send check or money order—no cash or CODs. Please allow 3-4 weeks for shipment.

Ms./Mrs./Mr._____

Address_____

City/State_____ Zip_____

Behold a bold new world of adventure

RACE AGAINST TIME

Jam-packed with danger, suspense, and intrigue, RACE AGAINST TIME pits teenage Stephen Lane and his handsome bachelor uncle, Richard, against ruthless enemies in exotic lands. Chased, trapped, and pushed to the edge of death, they *always* survive, due in no small part to their secret weapon—a pair of Kronom KD2 computer watches.

by J. J. Fortune $2.25 each

☐ 1	REVENGE IN THE SILENT TOMB	97707-X-35
☐ 2	ESCAPE FROM RAVEN CASTLE	92406-5-30
☐ 3	PURSUIT OF THE DEADLY DIAMONDS	97181-0-14
☐ 4	SEARCH FOR MAD JACK'S CROWN	97685-5-23
☐ 5	DUEL FOR THE SAMURAI SWORD	92172-4-24
☐ 6	EVIL IN PARADISE	92430-8-22
☐ 7	THE SECRET OF THE THIRD WATCH	97745-2-39
☐ 8	TRAPPED IN THE U.S.S.R.	99058-0-10
☐ 9	JOURNEY TO ATLANTIS	94272-1-37

At your local bookstore or use this handy coupon for ordering:

DELL READERS SERVICE—DEPT. R678B
P.O. BOX 1000, PINE BROOK, N.J. 07058

Please send me the above title(s). I am enclosing $_____ (please add 75¢ per copy to cover postage and handling). Send check or money order—no cash or CODs. Please allow 3-4 weeks for shipment. CANADIAN ORDERS: please submit in U.S. dollars.

Ms./Mrs./Mr._____

Address_____

City/State_____ Zip _____

LLOYD ALEXANDER

THE PRYDAIN CHRONICLES

The imaginary land of Prydain is beset by warlords and enchantresses, and the minions of death are gathering their forces. Into the battle comes young Taran, who seeks to test his manhood and discover his origins. The adventures of Taran and his companions unreel at a terrifying pace in the classic conflict of good vs. evil.

_____THE BOOK OF THREE, **$2.50**   90702-0

_____THE BLACK CAULDRON, **$2.95**   90649-0

_____THE CASTLE OF LLYR, **$2.95**   91125-7

_____TARAN WANDERER, **$2.95**   98483-1

_____THE HIGH KING,   **2.95**   93574-1

At your local bookstore or use this handy coupon for ordering:

Dell | **DELL BOOKS** R678C
P.O. BOX 1000, PINE BROOK, N.J. 07058-1000

Please send me the above title(s). I am enclosing $_____ (please add 75¢ per copy to cover postage and handling). Send check or money order—no cash or COOs. Please allow 3-4 weeks for shipment. <u>CANADIAN ORDERS</u>: please submit in U.S. dollars.

Ms./Mrs./Mr._____

Address_____

City/State_____ Zip_____

The reader is the hero

in the

FIGHTING FANTASY GAMEBOOKS

These exciting paperbacks—part story, part game—combine the best elements of *Dungeons and Dragons* and *Choose Your Own Adventure*. They feature score sheets, monster encounters, and elaborate combat systems played with a pair of dice and a pencil. The reader decides which route to take, which monsters to fight, and where to use his special knowledge of the magic arts. Books by Steve Jackson, Peter Andrew Jones, and/or Ian Livingstone.

_____STARSHIP TRAVELLER, $1.95   98241-3

_____THE WARLOCK OF FIRETOP MOUNTAIN, $1.95   99381-4

_____THE CITADEL OF CHAOS, $1.95   91280-6

_____THE FOREST OF DOOM, $1.95   92679-3

_____CITY OF THIEVES, $1.95   91374-8

_____DEATHTRAP DUNGEON, $2.25   91717-4

_____ISLAND OF THE LIZARD KING, $2.25   94027-3

Not available in Canada

At your local bookstore or use this handy coupon for ordering:

DELL READERS SERVICE—DEPT. R678D
P.O. BOX 1000, PINE BROOK, N.J. 07058

Please send me the above title(s). I am enclosing $_____ (please add 75¢ per copy to cover postage and handling). Send check or money order—no cash or COD5. Please allow 3-4 weeks for shipment.

Ms./Mrs./Mr._____

Address_____

City/State_____ Zip_____